The Subtle Thief

The Subtle Thief

A Desmond Fairbrother Mystery

Richard Wendorf

The Subtle Thief
Published by The Conrad Press Ltd. in the United
Kingdom 2023

Tel: +44(0)1227 472 874

www.theconradpress.com
info@theconradpress.com

ISBN 978-1-916966-07-9

Typesetting and cover design by Michelle Emerson
michelleemerson.co.uk

The Conrad Press logo was designed by Maria
Priestley

Printed and bound in Great Britain by Clays Ltd,
Elcograf S.p.A.

For James and BJ,
my favorite New Yorkers

Perhaps my semblance might deceive the truth,
That I to manhood am arriv'd so near.

John Milton, *Sonnet VII*

Tuesday, 4 September

What's a girl to do? He was late again — and for the second or third time this year. Fog over the home counties? Heightened security measures at Heathrow? Endangered species on the tarmac? Whatever the problem was, it had made a long day even longer for his Highness and a short wait a little longer for me.

I had hoped that Desi would take the morning or early afternoon flight from London – you know, like normal people do – but the Secretary of the Royal Academy had asked him to give a talk over tea on the day of his return, and Desi does just about anything not to disappoint his friends.

Although, in truth, to most of *my* friends his schedule during one of these forays sounds anything but grueling: lunch or dinner in his honor (honour, I suppose I should say), a lecture or master class at one of the libraries or museums, appointments with antiques and art dealers, and sometimes just enough time to make it to the theater or to Covent Garden. It's not unlike his life here in New York, of course, but my poor frequent flier normally returns exhausted as well as elated. ¡*Pobrecito!*

The phone finally rang at ten in the evening. 'So sorry, sweet Abby.' (He was certainly at his most apologetic.) 'A delay because of what the English politely call an "industrial action," which means, of course, that absolutely no action took place at all. But I'm now on the ground, I have my luggage, and I'm in a cab that will bring me brightly to your door, traffic willing. See you soon, Miss Abigail.'

'Forgiven, Dr. Fairbrother. Dinner awaits you, and much else as well.'

It wasn't, strictly speaking, my door. Not at all. It was Desi's door, through which his favorite cat burglar had entered an hour or two ago, ready to lay out a decidedly un-English dinner for his arrival. I had been to one of those overpriced food emporia on the Upper East Side – the kind of place that my friends and I collectively seem to keep in business – where I had selected fresh fettucini, plum tomatoes, basil, some local lettuces, a chunk of good *Parmigiano*, a medley of fresh fruits, and — to start — a mixture of olives, caperberries, and roasted sweet peppers.

One of the many wonders of Desi's over-the-top house is his over-the-top kitchen, which has been set up to accommodate a small army of caterers when he entertains. Given how miniscule my own kitchen in the city is, I shimmer with pleasure the minute I enter his, surrounded by more sinks, stoves, ovens, refrigerators, and copper pots than you'd find at an upscale kitchen store. Gleaming black tiles underfoot, of course, and two old kilims providing just the right amount of color on the floor. There is always champagne in the wine cooler, gin and vodka in the freezer, an assortment of vermouths in the refrigerator, a colorful selection of oils and vinegars on the counter — and plenty of room in which to make a proper mess, which suits me just fine.

Hanging on the only wall not entirely devoted to Lucullan endeavors is a vintage Warhol silkscreen print of Goethe in the *campagna*. I once suggested to Desi that it might have made better sense to hang a copy of Warhol's tomato soup can on that wall, but he was only slightly amused. And yet, if I could actually afford one of those blasted soup cans, it might be fun to substitute it the next time the master of the house goes traveling.

Having arranged and admired the fruits of my small spending spree, I'd cut the tomatoes in half and placed them in a roasting dish with olive oil, salt, pepper, garlic, and some dried oregano. Into the oven for half an hour or so, and then, when cooled, into the food processor to provide a light, early autumnal sauce for the fresh pasta. A colorful salad to follow would just about do the trick. And then some fruit with *crème fraîche* ladled on top. Champagne to accompany the berries and melons, a light red Rhone to go with the pasta and salad, and one of our favorite martinis to greet my traveler once he finally arrived. But which one? Decisions, decisions.

Desi prefers gin, Abby prefers vodka. One exquisite compromise is what Desi calls 'Brendan's Revenge' after his late father, a thirsty Chicagoan who loved gin even though gin never seemed to love him. No stirring or shaking necessary! You simply rub a wide piece of lemon peel on the inside of a martini glass, fill the glass with chilled vodka, and then float a capful of cold gin on top. It's amazing how pungent the gin is, how quickly it flavors the entire drink. On this particular night, however, there was no need for compromises. I mixed gin, a few drops of vermouth, ice, and the requisite peel of lemon in a sturdy cocktail shaker and placed it in the freezer until my scholar-gypsy eventually arrived *a casa*.

The doorbell finally rang, I pressed the buzzer in the hallway, and Desi was suddenly home, looking as if it were ten-forty in the evening in New York rather than almost four in the morning in London. After a long and hungry kiss I gave him an appreciative once-over. He looked fabulous, as always — the thinking woman's Pierce Brosnan, with silvering temples and a few

4

honorary degrees — and I naturally had to give him a hard time. 'My God, Desi, if it weren't for your suitcase, no one could tell that you've been traveling. Does business class now provide a dry-cleaning service?'

He gave me that weak smile of his, the one that reminds me that he doesn't like to be teased, but he looped his arm around my back and pulled me in. 'London was so hot this afternoon that I was a soggy mess by the time I arrived at the airport. So each time I took a walk to stretch on the plane, I changed one article of clothing — and presto, by the time I disembarked, I was almost a new man. What's for dinner?'

'Something much too good for you, so just be patient. In the meantime, here's something wicked straight from the freezer.'

I poured my icy concoction into two antique vessels, added a bit of ice, and we gently clinked our glasses together. 'You look great, Abby, a sight for two very sore eyes.'

'Yes I do, don't I?' It was also warm in New York, but not unseasonably so for early September, and I had therefore played one of my minimalist cards: black Capri pants, a red tank top with nothing under it, and some rather extravagant heels. 'What do you think of my elegant new shoes?'

'I think your elegant new shoes deserve to be grounded, banned from public scrutiny. They're too hot for even the hottest of those nightclubs you drag me to. Where in the world did you find them? Has Fredericks of Hollywood opened a boutique here in Manhattan?'

'They're you-know-whose, half-Czech, half-Spanish, one-hundred-percent sex.'

'Ah yes, you-know-whose. The one who says that "sex isn't that important, but good underwear is?"'

'Yup. I bought them on deep end-of-season discount. The devil made me do it.'

Desi kissed me again and then raised my tank top and placed his icy lips on my left nipple, warming and cooling it simultaneously.

'Equal time, please!'

After both of my tender buttons were fully stretched, he returned his mouth to mine and ran his hands lightly down the front and back of my tight and obliging capris. By this point it was, of course, our usual dilemma: instant gratification or prolonged provocation? I opted for the latter.

'Desi dearest, if you carry me up to the bedroom right now, you won't stay awake for the dinner I've slaved over for the past several days.'

'How many?'

'Three, at least. Maybe four. I've lost count it's been so long.'

And then he wisely set me free, picked up his drink, and announced that he was starving:

'You know that I can never eat anything on the

plane. I can't wait to see what you've been up to.'

'Soon enough,' I replied. 'Why don't you sit down and I'll refresh your glass.'

'And peel me a grape?'

'That comes later, with dessert — and champagne, if you have the staying power.'

With that he took his seat and eyed me with a deeply enigmatic smile. 'Did you get much writing done while I was gone? Or were you completely disconsolate?'

'Just a little — just a little writing, I mean. I spent some of the week researching an article for one of those fancy interior design magazines. They wanted a saucy take on someone's new apartment in Chelsea. A traditional place that has been transformed into a showcase for contemporary art. If you didn't spy the kitchen and bedrooms, you'd think that it was open to the public. You'll find it absolutely appalling.'

'What do you mean "I'll find it absolutely appalling"? Am I going there?'

'All in good time, buster. They're giving a party there and I'll need a bodyguard to protect me from the young male things in black and leather.'

'And the young female things in black and leather.'

'Those I can handle. Some of them have even read a novel, which does make it a bit easier to explain what I do for a living.'

He paused for just a moment. 'You've got a point. But even so, people go to cocktail parties here and ask each other what they do and where they live and which schools and colleges they've attended – it's quite normal. To ask any of those questions in England would be considered absolutely taboo. It would be like asking your hostess for the "bloody toilet" — although I'm not quite sure which of those two words is currently thought to be the more objectionable.'

'The fucking toilet? Surely that's worse.'

'Not really. The f-bomb is considered rather chic among the cultured and chattering classes these days.'

'So, then, what's the etiquette?'

'You're expected to know ahead of time.'

'But what if you don't know who's going?'

'There's an elaborate system of indirection. You might drop a name, for instance, in the lightest possible way, and see if that leads anywhere.'

'Christ, Desi. I think I'd rather go to this party in Chelsea than spend my time navigating the shoals of South Kensington.'

By this time I had drained the fettucine and arranged it smartly on two crisp white plates with an ample topping of basil, cheese, and the world's simplest red sauce. '*Tricolore*, Dottore Fairbrother! Do you wish to dine here at the island or out on the terrace?'

Desi opened the French doors that led to the walled garden at the back of the house and checked the temperature. 'Not terribly hot anymore, my sweet, but rather humid and still a bit buggy. Let's slum it and stay in the kitchen.'

Slum it! As if you could slum anything in this place.

Desi brought out two black placemats, gray linen napkins, and some lovely old silver.

'Not Italian, but it will do.'

And yes, he was hungry: two servings of pasta and even some compliments on my nervous lettuce and salad dressing, no less.

'So. You did enjoy your trip?'

'Of course I did,' he replied. 'There are so many Brits working as curators and museum directors here in the States that it's really quite gratifying to be asked to mentor the English on their own ground for a change. There seems to be a general realization that Americans are quite capable of saying a few intelligent things about British paintings. I had a leisurely dinner with Edward Pettigrew, and I was introduced to some interesting new people.'

'How is dear Edward?' Edward had been one of Desi's mentors years ago.

'Ageless, Abby; perfectly ageless.'

'And the highlight of your week?'

'I met some friends at the Savoy Grill last night. I haven't been there in years, perhaps even decades, and it really hasn't changed that much, even after spending a trillion dollars renovating it. Did you know that they used to have a seat reserved for the statue of a black cat so that there would never be thirteen guests at a table?'

'Somehow, knowing the English even a little bit, I can't say that I'm surprised. And the worst part?'

'No significant disappointments. Just the reality of traveling to and from London — and within London — with a vast army of Americans boasting cell phones, water bottles, and fanny packs.'

'Any novels in their pockets?'

'I don't think so. Just iPods.'

'*Mon Dieu!* We all have our work cut out for us. Are you ready for dessert?'

'Yes, I am. But would you mind terribly, Abby, if I took a quick shower? It would feel great at this point, perfect preparation for your champagne to follow.'

'*Your* champagne, Desi; I can't afford the labels you've got squirreled away here. But yes, of course, toddle off to your sanctum sanctorum and have a quick splash. I'll have dessert ready in ten minutes or so.'

And with that he was on his feet, clearing our makeshift table and lifting his handsome suitcase one more time.

'Wait a minute!' he said. 'I completely forgot.

I have some moveable feasts hidden in my luggage, no doubt approvingly sniffed by the patrol dogs at JFK.'

Out came one, then two, then three large wedges of English cheese. 'The first one is Cheshire, very hard to find the right kind over here. The second is a soft cheese, almost the consistency of clotted cream. And the third is my new favorite, Stinking Bishop.'

'Stinking Bishop?'

'I'm afraid so: great name, great cheese. Why don't you have a taste while I shower; it will do you good.'

And so I did, for it certainly didn't need any airing! In fact, I wondered what the rest of Desi's belongings would smell like after spending half a day in close proximity to this particular man of the cloth. And that in turn reminded me of the wonderful chapter devoted to the disposition of cheese in *Three Men in a Boat* (*To Say Nothing of the Dog*), which my father loved to read to us when we were children. But I digress. You'll have to blame it on my itinerant friend — to say nothing of the cheese, which was really, really good.

Ten minutes passed, then fifteen. I had the fruit course ready and had uncorked the shamelessly expensive champagne, but there was still no sign — or sound — of Desi. So I decided to look for him, ascending the gleaming white staircase to the second floor and walking through the open door to the only bedroom. Almost everything about this unusual house has been executed on a grand scale: the living room, the library, the kitchen, even the master bathroom. The only exception is Desi's bedroom, to which he gave more modest proportions when he reconfigured the building several years ago.

The walls here are painted a soft green with hints of gray and blue. There are no bookcases, only a collection of black and red antique Chinese cabinets, including one on each side of the bed.

Antique Chinese lamps, black African bowls, and a variety of small bronzes rest on top of these bureaus, and Piranesi's four etchings of fanciful *grotteschi* are beautifully set off against the soothing walls. This is the only room in the house with carpeting, which looks and feels like soft sisal. The bed is simply tailored in Italian silks and cottons, with a handsome headboard to match. Above the headboard, a fabulous starburst mirror that Desi bought in the south of France and precariously transported back to New York. And on top of the bed, completely naked, lying on his stomach, I discovered the master of the house himself, looking as if dessert and champagne — not to mention more serious pursuits — were no longer on the day's agenda. But there was only one way to make sure.

I quietly kicked off my heels, peeled off my

tank top and trousers, and made my way up from the bottom of the bed, softly rubbing his calves, thighs, and buns and then placing a chaste kiss on his exposed cheek. Then a less chaste kiss in his ear, on his neck, and down his long, lean back. His dark blond hair was a bit damp and he was still deeply tanned from our time on Long Island. As I raised his hips slightly and pulled his crown jewels back between his legs, I heard a small but distinct expression of pleasure. His cock immediately stiffened in my hand, even more so once I applied my expert lip-service to it and ran my fingertips between his smooth buns. How long could he hold out, I wondered? And then, a few minutes later, I quickly found out as his entire body flexed and he allowed himself to explode.

When I was finished, I kissed him on the cheek, slowly crept off the bed, placed a light blanket on top of him and, giving him a tender glance, shut the door quietly behind me. The champagne downstairs made a perfect chaser.

Friday, 7 September

I didn't see Desi again 'til Friday. Since getting back he was swamped with engagements as the new cultural season got underway, and I, for my part, was once again absorbed in my *nouveau roman* as well as my little architectural essay. It's pretty easy for me to allow myself to be distracted from my work – especially when Desi's around – so I wanted to make the best of my time alone. Truth is, I made fuck-all progress on the novel and dreaded a call from my agent, which I expected at any moment. Everything they say about writing a second or third novel is true – it's absolute torture!

On Friday, however, Desi hosted one of his trademark parties and I happily attended as his *agent provocateur*, as he likes to put it, which helped me to recover my spirits. The Frick Collection was hosting a symposium for younger scholars and Desi offered to give a cocktail party and buffet dinner afterwards for forty or fifty guests. There would be the scholars themselves, some of their teachers, the heads of various foundations, a few scholarly publishers, a strong representation from local libraries and museums, a handful of Frick trustees and major benefactors, and the curious creatures I like to describe as the blue-rinse set.

Desi likes to tease me about some of my wilder friends, referring to them as denizens of New York's *demi-monde* (or worse) — but honestly, they are nothing compared to the characters who turn up to drink Desi's wine, inhale his food, and drool over the objects in his collection. They are a strange group of ageing beauties of both genders and various sexual orientations, who travel from one party to another, get off on each other's company and vanity in an almost frantic way, and lap up the gorgeousness of he who is Desmond Fairbrother. They're not entirely freeloaders, however. Some of them will host similar parties later in the season, and some of the collectors among them have been very generous to Desi. Desi has admirers of all kinds — some of them young, many of them his own age — but no one is as fervid in his or her adoration as these well-coiffed guests, these Dorian and Dorothea Grays.

I arrived a few minutes early to offer whatever assistance I could as Desi gave his final orders to the caterers, servers, and bartenders. But everything was, as usual, in impeccable order, including some beautiful flower arrangements from Desi's favorite supplier around the corner. I relaxed, asked for a spritzer, and surveyed the premises.

The history of this particular building is not entirely clear, but it seems as if it began life as a carriage house at the turn of the twentieth century, with real carriages and horses — and presumably lowly retainers overhead, if that's the oxymoronic image I'm looking for. It was then turned into a garage in the 1920s — and what a garage it must have been, with concrete floors and drains for water and oil — before being converted into a single-family residence in the 1940s and then, in the late '60s, purchased by an art collector in pursuit of 'clean, modern space.' Well, she certainly got it!

When Desi took over the ownership almost thirty years later, it was badly in need of rehabilitation, which is just the kind of challenge he unfortunately relishes. No architects were officially taken on, of course, although Desi consulted a number of his friends and worked with a very knowledgeable contractor. The essential problem was one of proportion: the structure was wide enough and unusually deep, but the ceilings were much too low. Desi's solution was about as radical as it could be. Instead of making a series of adjustments, he raised the ceiling of the entire first floor and left the center of the building completely open, with a grand staircase leading up to the bedroom and library above. He placed the modest bedroom over the kitchen, with a view down to the terrace in back; he built the large library over the living room, with a view down to the street below. Next to the bedroom he created a spiffy spa, with an open shower, an oversized soaking tub, his and her sinks, a small sauna, and skylights above. This hidden gem opens only onto the bedroom; everyone else must use the guest bath below, which is large enough to house a collection of old-master prints on its walls and a humongous mirror from the waning days of the *ancien régime*.

Most of the first floor, however, is devoted to the atrium that contains the dramatic staircase and to the oversized living room at the front of the house. This is where Desi has placed most of his collection of paintings, statuary, and furniture. It is, if I do say so myself, an eclectic gathering, but the pairings work well together and the space itself — painted a warm taupe, beautifully illuminated, and grand in scale — projects a sense of what my glossy interiors magazine would call 'refined masculinity.' Yes, I think those are the words I want. I may not be able to hold a party in the classical wing of the Met, but I can certainly do so in Desmond Fairbrother's carriage house, which provides many of the same decorative and aesthetic elements. Both the living room and the atrium are punctuated by Roman statues: busts on marble columns as well as several full-sized figures that provide a sense of movement within the rooms. Above the fireplace in the living room Desi has placed his largest painting, an allegorical composition by Angelica Kauffman, with the artist herself appearing as *Pittura*. Crisply tailored chairs and an oversized Sarouk rug have been placed in front of the fireplace. Across the room stands one of several Italian tables, this one with antique uprights carved from Travertine and a large sheet of glass perched on top. This is where the buffet will be laid out. (There is no bar, by the way. My darling thinks they are unsightly and prefers to have waiters ask his guests what they'd like to drink.) Desi has hung two Italian landscapes here, and elsewhere there are Venetian scenes by Guardi, a small Constable, and an oil on copper by Canaletto. Most of the other paintings are portraits, including what Desi describes as an acceptable depiction of a young scholar by Reynolds.

There's also a small Fragonard and an unusual head and shoulders by Lawrence that I find interesting because the artist decided not to finish any of the usual background elements. There's not a single book in view (they're all upstairs in the library, where they should be), nor any other visual distraction. Is it missing anything, I once asked him? Only a landscape by Poussin, Desi confided, but someday that will find its way here too, I imagine.

Desi was very much in his element, rested and almost relaxed. I was pleased to see that he was wearing the lapis-and-gold cufflinks I had given him for his most recent birthday. He had changed his clothing and was wearing his normal evening outfit, a navy suit with a white shirt and a simple tie of woven silk. 'We all have our uniforms,' he is fond of saying; 'mine happens not to be black.' During the day he usually chooses a gray suit and a blue shirt with white collar and cuffs. He wears slipper-like loafers at all times, suede during the day, velvet in the evening. And lord help us, no initials! 'The important thing is to keep matters simple,' he says. 'Remember the immortal words of the much maligned Duke of Windsor: "Dress soft."' Much maligned for good reason, I always mumble to myself.

I, for one, don't dress soft — and I normally wear black. Black punctuated by red, to be precise. So tonight I put on a fairly simple sable dress, coral earrings and necklace, red nail polish, and another pair of stilettos, standing proudly above their vibrant red soles. 'You look fabulous,' Desi whispered as he kissed me. 'And I think I owe you a raincheck.'

'Thank you, you're sweet — and' (with a smile) 'you owe me much more than a mere raincheck, whatever that means.'

'Let's put you on display directly in front of darling Angelica.'

'No Lily Bart for me tonight, mister. I don't do the *tableau vivant* thing, remember? I could easily find you a pliant model or actress, however, if that's what you're looking for these days.'

'To be honest, Abby, an actress or a model might be a welcome change after all the curatorial types we'll soon be awash in. Is it time to trade in that glass of yours, by the way? You might want to fortify yourself before all of my friends arrive.'

We both ordered a Negroni from the waiter and sat down on an antique sofa that Desi had reupholstered. 'So whom should I focus on this evening, Dr. Fairbrother? Do you have any potential clients in mind?' Desi makes his money (as if he needs it) by helping people to navigate the art world.

'As you well know, sweetheart, in my world everyone is a potential client, I suppose. You never know who will want advice — and actually compensate you for it. We should pay attention to the trustees and other heavy rollers, of course, but sometimes a commission comes right out of the blue, from someone you couldn't possibly imagine would want to build a serious collection.'

This is Desi through and through. Despite his refined tastes, one of the things I love about him is that he's not a snob. A good eye is a good eye, whoever it belongs to.

'I met some brash young financial whiz,' he continued, 'at a party earlier this week who took me aside to ask if I knew anything about Meissen. And not just Meissen, mind you, but the very earliest stuff, the elusive *Böttgerware* made out of red clay. I was really astonished: was it a sign that civilization as we know it has not entirely disappeared?'

'I doubt it — unless he asked you about the novels you've been reading as well.' And then I couldn't resist: 'I hate to ask you this, Desi, but *do* you know anything about early Meissen?'

'More than he does, I'm happy to say, and in a week's time I shall be a proper Meissen-meister. It's important to know things, of course, but it's also important to know where to find them.'

'And do you?'

'All in good time.'

At which point one of the large case clocks struck seven and the first silver-haired guests made their way through the front door: sleek, tanned, and ready to party. Among them, I was pleased to see, was Robert Linardo, a collector and decorator who worked with Desi when he redesigned the carriage house and who has remained a close friend of ours. Robert is a true taste-maker, someone with a signature style that others often try to emulate. He is elegant and courtly, always sporting a small flower in his

21

lapel, always boasting a wave of silver hair that would have put Liberace to shame, and always flirting outrageously with the women — which is always easier to carry off if you play for the opposite team.

Robert kissed me and darlinged me, told me how much he wished he could wear shoes as edgy as mine, and then introduced me to his immaculately turned-out companions: two Park Avenue dowagers, a few fellow boulevardiers, and one of the museum's trustees. After giving them a full dose of Abby at her very best, I looked around to see if there was anyone in the room besides myself under the age of forty. An assistant curator? An assistant professor? Perhaps even a genuine graduate student? As luck would have it, my wishes were answered in the form of a beaming David Lundgren, one of Desi's favorite younger colleagues at the Met and a participant in the symposium earlier in the day.

'My God, Abby, I'm glad to see someone I know. You look terrific, as always. Is Desmond giving you all the attention you deserve?'

'To be honest, David, I think you've seen more of his Highness this week than I have. How is life at the museum?'

'I love it, I really do. People want to commiserate with me because it's an entry-level position but it's really the perfect job for me. All day long I get to look at beautiful paintings and

22

meet fascinating people. As we say in the Midwest, I'm in hog heaven.'

'Somehow, David, that doesn't quite ring true for the Baroque painting galleries, though if memory serves me right, you do have those Tiepolos – probably the closest you get to paradise!'

'*Touché*, Abby. Very quick off the mark. And I forgot to put on my protective armor at the door.'

'Serves you right. But tell me, how did your presentation go today, as if I have to ask?'

'Pretty well, I think,' he said. 'I gave my lecture without too much anxiety, and there were some good questions afterwards. There were even a few compliments as we left the Frick, but you never know who's sharpening his or her dagger in the last row, including some of the people I work with at the Met. That's the one thing I don't like about museum work, everyone's so territorial about their specialty.'

'Or sub-specialty, I imagine. But I really can't believe that anyone would wish you harm, David. You *are* speaking rhetorically, right?'

'Of course, Abby.'

'And there are turf wars everywhere. You haven't lived until your new novel has been reviewed by your fellow-novelists, believe me. They make the regular book reviewers look like Golden Retriever puppies.'

'I know I shouldn't ask, but are you making

headway on the new one?'

'No, it's fine to ask; it's going as well as can be expected, and if I hit a dry patch I can always write something else — something that people might even want to read.'

'Oh come on, Abby.'

'No really, it's fine. I enjoy a little frivolous journalism.'

'For the magazines?'

'*Exactement*. Although I suppose that I should be blogging as well. Do you have museum blogs you look at?'

'I used to, but you have no idea how much time people waste reading those things. If I were their boss, I'd certainly try to rein them in.'

'They don't have enough time, darling. They're too busy blogging themselves.'

'So, did I get an answer from you about your new book?'

'Sorry, sweetheart; I'm not trying to be evasive. I've actually written several chapters and have a decent sense of where I'm headed — although it won't be a surprise to any of my readers, God knows.'

'Intergenerational conflict in old New England families?'

'You've got to write about what you know about, true or not false?'

'I should hope so, Abby. So here's a trick that one of my mentors in Chicago taught me: never publish anything about a picture before you've read the essay back to the painting itself. He really meant it: stand in front of the painting and put your writing on trial. You'd be amazed by what you learn from such a simple exercise.'

'Lucky you, though, David. You've got the paintings right on the premises. What about everyone else?'

'The principle's the same even if you have to rely on facsimiles. If you're going to make an extended argument, make sure that it's grounded in careful observation of the object itself.'

'Is this the kind of thing you can say at one of these symposia?'

'Good God, no! If I did, I'd lose my head in the culture wars. I find it better to preach privately and to practice publicly.'

'Nicely put — and not a bad lesson for all of us, come to think of it.'

Sweet David Lundgren, I thought. One of my favorite people, and Desi's, too. So what do we know about him?

He grew up in Minnesota, attended a very conservative fundamentalist college, and then blossomed as a graduate student in Chicago, both as a promising art historian and as a young man who took the very difficult step of uncloseting himself there. It wasn't easy for him, nor his family, but they are all good people and in due course they made their accommodations   with each other. And now here he was at the Met, devoting his career to Rubens and Van Dyck and Tiepolo, and making the most of life in New York. More power to him, as my father might well say.

'Hello, David! This party should be in celebration of you,' Desi said as he made his way over to the two of us. 'Your talk was excellent, arguably the best of the lot, but don't repeat that to anyone else in the room.'

'Thanks, Desmond. It means a lot to hear it from you — and to hear it here, surrounded by so many beautiful things and so many beautiful people.'

'Speaking of all the beautiful people,' Desi replied, 'I must continue to circulate, but let's try to have some time together when things are a bit more quiet.'

'Desmond,' I added, 'let's invite David to Sag Harbor next weekend. Are you free?'

'I certainly am — and I'd be delighted.'

'Perfect. Bring a friend — if you have one.' I gave him a kiss and began to look for Desi again. He was surrounded by a cluster of attractive women, all of them laughing in unison. I thought of joining them, but then thought better of it, preferring to order a glass of wine and survey the crowd, which had already swelled to its full complement. And what a God-awful pageant was now in view! The young scholars, of course, darkly dressed, tightly tailored, and desperately wondering when they could begin to relax. The professional class, obliged to shake hands and make small talk with everyone before they finally decided it was possible to depart. And then the social elite — the museum's trustees, other generous donors, members of Desi's blue-rinse set — who seemed, in all honesty, to be the only people truly enjoying themselves.

As the crowd began to thin a bit, some of our host's admirers began to demand more personalized attention, particularly a youngish Asian woman — a curator, no doubt — whom I had not seen before. She had jet-black hair, cut fairly short, and was wearing a red silk dress and black slides. She was thin, elegant, someone whom I was sure we (or at least Desi) would see again. But there were other contenders as well, especially two well-buffed women in their early sixties who seemed intent on enticing Desi to some other function later in the evening. My hunch was confirmed as his nibs slowly extricated himself and made his way across the room to me.

'Well, Abby, how are you putting up with the wildlife? Have you met anyone interesting?'

'Isn't everyone interesting by definition at one of your *soirées*, my dear?'

'No, but they certainly think they are, and that's half the battle, I suppose.'

'Well, I haven't met anyone who isn't a member of your extended fan club, and I see at least one debutante in red silk who must be among your newer members.'

'Susan Kim, just arrived at the Met from Cleveland, with what I understand is a well-deserved promotion to associate curator here. I'm encouraging her to get to know David, who can introduce her to some of her younger colleagues.'

I gave him my most loving, most entirely understanding smile. 'And I'm sure you can introduce her to many other things as well, Dr. Fairbrother.'

'I'm sure I can, Abby, but here's the issue at hand. My friends Betsy and Eleanor are about to give a little party afterwards at their club, and I'm wondering if you'd like to join me. They're very amusing, and you might possibly find it to be fun.'

'Sounds like work to me, partner. If you don't mind, I think I'll hold on to my raincheck.'

'Of course; I'll call you in the morning.'

A few minutes later he bade farewell to the last of his guests, kissed me goodbye on the sidewalk, and joined his friends in Betsy's limousine. As the long black beast made its way down the street, I wasn't surprised to catch a glimpse of red silk in the back seat.

Sunday, 9 September

'I just don't get it, Abby.' This was Renata, one of my college roommates and still my closest friend, enjoying a leisurely brunch with me on the Sunday. 'You're smart, you're attractive, you're successful. You've got a bit of money. You come from a distinguished old family. You could have any man you want — let me repeat — any man you want in New York City. Instead, you've *not* got Desmond Fairbrother. I don't get it.'

This is Conversation Number Three with Renata. Conversations Numbers One and Two — if you're interested — focus on my clothing ('Why so much red and black? Have you got some kind of crush on Stendhal?') and my anxiety over my career as a novelist ('Why don't you write something that will interest Hollywood and make you some real money?'). And so I adopted my infinitely patient look and began, once again, to relate the facts of life as I know them.

'First of all, Renata, neither of us wants to be

tied down. No hostages to fortune and all that kind of thing. He needs his own space and he wants it to reflect who he is. I feel perfectly happy being there, being part of his world, but if I moved in it would be the kiss of death for both of us. And let's not even talk about marriage!

'Second, I need my own freedom as well. A room of my own, as your good friend Virginia Woolf once said. Writing is solitary work. I need a quiet place where I can write just as much as I need the company and stimulation of other people. And I absolutely don't need someone else dictating a schedule to me. No matter how disciplined you try to be, writing comes when it comes. You can't force it, and you can't simply drop it when your juices are flowing and someone is calling you to dinner. Desmond understands this. When we do get together, it's without pencils and laptops. I don't write — and, except when he's giving his parties, he doesn't pursue his business either.'

'Whatever *that* is,' she interjected, not for the first time.

'And Renata dearest, as you of all people know, we both enjoy our little sexual adventures, at least in a modest kind of way. We enjoy each other, but we like the occasional challenge as well.'

'But if you're honest, aren't you just a little bit jealous of his other conquests? What about that

Asian doll you've just told me about?'

'Not really. And neither is he jealous of my occasional trophy. The adventures keep us sharp; they keep us on our toes. And besides, it's rather flattering to be the central figure in the life of a man who could have virtually any woman in Manhattan — and the Bronx and Staten Island, too.'

'Not everyone, Abby. He's a bit on the epicurean side for me.' Epicurean? I had to give Renata a few points for that one – and if I'm really being honest, I have to admit to feeling a small twinge of jealousy when I notice his attention turning to someone new.

But I tried once again: 'Come on, Renata, that's exactly what makes him attractive to so many other people: his ability to look and listen more carefully than other people do.'

'That and being a connoisseur of mattresses as well as paintings and sculpture?'

'He's a connoisseur of women, if that's what you mean.'

'And the occasional man, I seem to remember. And what about the famous sauna?'

'I didn't realize that it was famous.'

'All right, Abby, I guess we can't go there, but someday maybe you'll spill the beans. If not to Renata, who else?'

It's true. Renata and I have been very close for many years — how many I won't say, but we're both still junior fellows at the Morgan Library with a couple of years to spare. She's part of a small clutch of female friends who trail each other from the city to the country and back again.

Renata is also a genuine New Yorker: born and bred on this small island, city-smart, a little skeptical about anything that sounds too good to be true. Except for those four years spent with me in chilly Cambridge, she's made New York her home, forging her way in public relations and still looking for the right guy. She married early, an attractive classmate who specialized in mergers and acquisitions back when there were still companies with which to merge. But a few years later he decided on a new acquisition of his own, and Renata (never one to do things by halves) negotiated a divorce settlement that took even my breath away. I've introduced her to several of my male friends — and a few of Desi's — but no one so far has quite clicked.

Of course I've sometimes wondered exactly what Desi thinks of Renata: she's attractive after all, she's got good taste, and her job has put her in touch with a number of interesting people. But I never dwell on such things. What would be the point?

In all fairness it's clear that Desi is drawn to women who have a sense of personal style, a sense (as we used to say) that they are comfortable in their own skin — or leather, or fur, or loft, or (in Renata's case) a classic pre-war six. The connoisseurship he practices is a special way of knowing: partly intuitive, but firmly based on years of study and intelligent looking — educating the eye more than anything else. Of course he's opinionated, but I've rarely seen him be overbearing or rude, and he doesn't make hasty judgments, even about the truly annoying people I've introduced him to.

Renata, I'm happy to say, doesn't fit into this last category, but she and Desi have never entirely hit it off. She may be a little high-strung for Desi — high maintenance, as we used to say. In any case, she's a member of my fan club even if she isn't entirely one of his; and Desi, who is the most imperturbable person I know, is more than happy to be in Renata's company, even for a long stretch in the country, where I hoped she too would be joining us the following weekend.

'Abby?'

'Yes, sweetie.' Lunch was behind us and we were slowly making our way through the rites of espresso.

'Maybe I'm just jealous of your relationship with Desmond in some strange way — and perhaps of your sexual attitudes as well. But I was really very happy being married, you know, and I'd like to think that the stability of marriage and children is still a real possibility for me.'

'Well, I think I'd choose a rather different

word for it, *chiquita*: not so much stability as a complicated balancing act? But why not? You've certainly got room for it all.' To say the least! She even has room for a live-in nanny or two. As I said, it was quite a settlement.

'And if you and Desmond ever *did* decide on monogamous cohabitation with offspring, he has quite the place himself!' She was teasing, of course.

As for my own little Desmonds and Abigails, I seem to be getting by quite happily without them. It helps, of course, that my siblings are populating New England with a bumper crop of Higginsons, thus simultaneously pleasing my parents and allowing me to spoil the little buggers whenever possible. I never could have imagined myself in the role of fairy godmother, but there I occasionally am, hamsters and bedtime stories at the ready.

Renata was in love with the carriage house and had been curious about how Desi had come by it, at presumably no little cost to him. But that had been a bit disingenuous of her, as I'd explained at the time that Desi's family was comfortably off back in Chicago, but they certainly weren't rich, and God knows the life of an assistant professor doesn't easily produce carriage houses or underwrite charity events. The truth was that a client had left the house to Desi, deciding that no one else would make better use of it. It was essentially a question of taste — and I suppose one of control as well. Desi's friend had no close relatives, and she thought that it made better sense to leave the property to someone who had helped shape her collection rather than bequeath it to her alma mater, which would immediately put it on the market. So she left her art collection to the Museum of Modern Art and a few other places, established a scholarship fund at her college, and virtually overnight made Desi a reasonably wealthy man and the owner of one of the most unusual houses in New York.

'They must have been very good friends.'

Renata's emphasis was firmly on the 'very.'

I'd considered taking the proverbial end run on this one, but then decided to dive straight ahead, if I may mix my athletic metaphors. 'Yes, they were very good friends, and he was quite devoted to her. But you know what happened once word got out about the carriage house. Other friends decided to give Desmond things as well. A painting here, a lovely piece of sculpture there, because they knew that Desmond would take good care of their things. And eventually, of course, they will all make their way to the appropriate institution. But meantime everything is beautifully showcased: the old with the new, East with West, the fine arts with the decorative arts. Everything looking as if it had found a comfortable home. And it *is* a home, you know.

35

It's where he works and entertains —'

'—and takes in poor Abby from time to time?'

'Oh stop it, Renata. Enough is enough. The point I'm trying to make is that all of these nice people —'

'—nice rich people, you mean, with plenty of liquid assets.'

'Of course they're rich. But what's important is that all of these people share a basic trust in Desmond. They trust his taste, they trust his integrity, they trust his ability to make a collection of beautiful and unusual objects into a welcoming home —a place where they feel stimulated as well as comfortable.'

'I'm sorry, Abby. I didn't mean to put you on the defensive. Desmond has a real talent, no doubt about it. I could learn a thing or two from you guys. Perhaps I should join you when Desmond is hosting one of his fancy shindigs.'

'Of course you should,' I replied. 'He just gave a party for the Frick on Friday with all kinds of people eating and drinking him out of the proverbial. At least it's a tax deduction — or at least I hope it is! I've never seen so much wine and food consumed so quickly by so few people. But it was one of the first events of the season, and perhaps spending three months on the Vineyard or in the Hamptons has sharpened everyone's appetite.'

'The horrible Hamptons! That's certainly one

topic on which Desmond and I completely agree. Oh to be locked in traffic on the Montauk Highway every morning, afternoon, and evening. I don't understand why New Yorkers would flock to Long Island in order to sit in the same gridlock they enjoy every day of the week right here!'

'And Sag Harbor?'

'It's not officially part of the Hamptons in my view,' she responded.

'So if I invited you for a long weekend with Desmond and a few smart young things you'd think about coming?'

'Sure, Abby. But can you please throw in a few men our own age as well?'

'It's a deal, pal. I'm already working on it.'

And with that we went our separate ways, she further north, I a bit to the east. Well, quite a bit to the east. My *pied à terre* in the city is a small condominium just a few yards west of First Avenue. When my grandmother died a few years ago, all of us received rather more of an inheritance than we had anticipated. Thank God for those frugal Yankees! I used most of mine to buy my house in Sag Harbor, but there was enough left over, combined with some welcome book royalties, to purchase my little cocoon on the Upper East Side.

For several years home was a rather chic studio apartment in a high-rise building overlooking the Park, but I found that the view –

all right, it was extraordinary – was just too much of a distraction from *l'ecriture*. The entire world was literally at my feet when I was trying to create my own world, line by line, and I found it hard to concentrate up there, no matter how attractive the apartment otherwise was.

Then I got a tip-off from an editor friend who had been renting an apartment in an unusual building on a side street in Lenox Hill. It was unusual because it had very little presence on the sidewalk itself, just a small gateway that led to a quiet courtyard in front of a four-story building that stretched away from the street. All of the other houses on the block were brownstones with small gardens or terraces in back, and thus most of the units in my friend's building actually had a rather bucolic view. Not quite *Rear Window*, but a steady parade of dogs, children, sun-worshipers, and garden shears. It was really very charming, a quiet refuge in an otherwise bustling section of the city.

When the owner of the building decided to convert the apartments into condominiums, my friend decided that she wanted a larger place and happily arranged for me to purchase her studio. The location and the view were perfect — and I didn't want or need anything more substantial — but the unit itself needed more than a little TLC. It actually needed a complete makeover — and so did I, for the furniture that worked rather well in an international-style skyscraper was not going to fare very well in a second-story walkup.

Enter Desmond Fairbrother.

We stripped the wallpaper and sanded the floors – I'm speaking figuratively here, of course, for we had a gem of a contractor – removed the mismatched moldings and the faux fireplace, and opened up the small kitchen so that it looked directly onto the living room. Desi's stroke of genius, however (and he does occasionally have them), was to turn this fairly large studio into a one-bedroom by having a small sleeping loft built above the kitchen, cantilevered out over part of the main room. Although I lost a bit of space on the ground floor where we needed to erect a small circular staircase, the apartment was tall enough to accommodate the loft and still provide me with enough room for a set of tall bookcases. We painted these black, and they look terrific against the warm red walls. I placed an antique desk between the two tall windows overlooking the gardens below; the only other pieces of furniture are a small sofa, two comfortable chairs, a Lucite coffee-table, and a large, warm Heriz on the floor. On the walls I've arranged several black-and-white prints that I chose with a little help from my friend: a Hockney, a Picasso, an Ensor, a Gramaire, a Matisse, a Zorn, a Kollwitz, and (my favorite) a stunning impression of Bresdin's exotic camel in the desert.

This is a space that is both warm and serene at the same time. I don't use it for entertaining — not even for hosting Desi or Renata. There are bars and restaurants for those purposes, some of them only a stone's throw from here. This is a place in which to sleep, and read, and write. If it weren't for the laptop, the audio system, and an obscenely expensive coffeemaker, my small jolly corner could pass for a writer's studio a century or so ago. It's located a mere six blocks from the carriage house, it's all mine — and it suits me just fine, thank you very much.

Friday - Saturday, 15-16 September

I took the train out to East Hampton on Friday morning, which gave me plenty of time to run my usual errands. I'm in Sag Harbor on most weekends and pretty hard to miss as I drive about in my dashing ladybug — red body, black convertible top — with flowers, fresh bread, and groceries in the back seat and, on this occasion, one of my neighbor's Labradors accompanying me in front. I've been here long enough to be recognized in most of the local stores and I'm known to a fair number of the locals, too. It feels very much like home by now, perhaps because it looks so much like the New England villages that lie only a few miles north on the other side of the Sound.

I settled on the town first, before there was anything available to buy there, and it took me a long time to find exactly the right house — and when I did find it, it took me just as long to make it right for me. Or for anyone else, for that matter, because although it had those proverbial lovely bones, it was desperately in need of a facelift. I was seduced, however, by the fact that it had its own name. It was Captain Logan's house, named after an intrepid nineteenth-century mariner who plied the waters off the eastern seashore. I was even able to trace a bit of his personal saga at the local historical society, and getting to know Jeremiah Logan and his wife Louisa and their two daughters — even at a distance of two hundred years — turned out to be a psychological tonic as I spent increasing amounts of time (and money) cajoling my contractor and his colleagues to return the captain's house to its former glory.

The most recent owners, I discovered, had essentially camped out in it for over a decade, preferring to live with leaks and drafts and proprietary mice rather than ask the local bank for a home-equity loan. And so the task of restoring and refurbishing it fell squarely on you-know-whose two shoulders, a task made all the more difficult because no part of the house was habitable during the year-long process of gutting and rebuilding it. I guess you could say that it was an act of love — and faith — but there were certainly moments when I felt that I had made a huge (and expensive) mistake.

I put all of that behind me, however, the minute my long-suffering contractor placed the keys in my hand and invited me to inspect the final fruits of his handiwork. I soon had to admit that it's genuinely satisfying to see a neglected and seriously compromised building brought back to its original beauty. Captain Logan's house is not nearly as grand as many other buildings erected by prosperous merchants and seafarers during the golden age of sail; Sag Harbor is filled with them. But its proportions are right, the location is quiet, and the lawn and gardens are just small enough to manage on the weekends. There is, in fact, no front lawn to tend at all: just a semi-circular driveway of crushed stone with an entrance and an exit through a white picket fence. Around the driveway and in front of the house I've planted a small jungle of hydrangeas of all varieties, but always with blue and white flowers.

The house itself has a Greek-revival façade — very simple, with stately columns and handsome pilasters — and the exterior is painted a warm gray with white trim. The inside of the house is pretty much as it was: a double Queen Anne staircase once you step inside, a small drawing room on each side, and a decent-sized dining room behind them. My only innovation has been to demolish a series of run-on rooms at the back of the house, where I now have a proper kitchen and an informal dining space that looks out onto the terrace, the lap pool, and a yard about the size of a postage stamp. As I said, there's not much to tend. The priorities here are reading, swimming, entertaining, and enjoying our extended and sometimes complicated network of friends, who generally fit into the bedrooms on the second and third floors. Most of those rooms would be filled this weekend.

I met Desi at the station late in the afternoon. He looked a bit tired, but he was in good spirits and pleased to be lugging his own contribution to the festivities, a case of wine divided — not quite evenly, I was happy to see — between rosé for Saturday lunch and Bordeaux for dinner that evening.

'Are you ready for the onslaught, Abby? You look surprisingly perky to me.'

'I'm better than perky, Dr. Fairbrother.' I gave him a quick kiss once he had stowed his bags and wine and fastened his seatbelt. 'Here's a little welcome for you, darling.' I handed him a small sprig of flowers I'd tied in a posey.

'You sweetheart! The joy of the intense, clean smell of freesia. Are there more of these at home?'

'They're all over the place. Don't you wish someone would just bottle this smell and sell it as a perfume?'

'A lovely thought, but perhaps not quite on track.'

Merde! I could tell from the tone of his voice that I was about to be on the receiving end of a mini-lecture.

'Your problem is that flowers have relatively simple fragrances — one soft or pungent blast —

44

whereas perfume and eau de toilette are made up of several intertwining scents: top notes, heart notes, and base notes. Perfumes are a bit like red wine: they're sophisticated blends of merlot, cabernet sauvignon, and cabernet franc that distinguish one vintner from another. It's all rather French. But we Americans are so uncouth that we don't appreciate the subtlety. How many times have you heard "One merlot, please, bartender, and make it straight up."'

'Okay, okay, I get the point, *mon professeur*. Could we compromise and bottle it as room spray?'

'Of course you could. I think they call it *l'ambiance*.'

'No, Desi, you *know* they call it *l'ambiance*. But you're sweet to pretend you don't.'

My peripheral vision isn't terribly good, but I could see that he was smiling as we enjoyed the short ride to my house in the late-afternoon sun. He placed his hand on my right thigh and kissed me just below the ear. 'Hmmm, lavender with a hint of heliotrope? You smell almost as good as the freesia, Abby.'

'No, I smell even better. I'm a complicated blend, after all, to be enjoyed right away, a little bit later, and then later still. If I can keep you up that late, of course.'

'I'm looking forward to it. We've got the entire house to ourselves until the hordes arrive for lunch tomorrow, no?'

'Absolutely, and the night is young.'

After a swim, I grabbed a bottle of ice-cold vodka from the freezer, cut some strips of lemon zest, and mixed them together in two old champagne flutes: strong stuff, but we might just need it.

Desi kissed the back of my neck, ran his fingers lightly over my nipples, and rubbed his stiff cock against my buns and lower back. Orgasms are great, I thought to myself, but this fabulous moment, when everything is (literally!) yet to come, is pretty hard to beat.

Desi grinned as I clasped my arms around his neck. 'If we're very careful, Abby, I can deliver both you and the two drinks upstairs without spilling a drop.'

He was true to his word – and to all of his other promises as well.

In the morning, of course, we had to prepare ourselves for the house party that would begin to unfold around noontime. The cast of characters was still a bit uncertain. I had arranged to meet Renata at the station. David Lundgren was showing up with a friend — although who it was we didn't yet know. Odd that he should be secretive, but perhaps that was a result of years of being deep inside the closet. I was curious, though – would it be one of his new Met friends or someone he had been keeping to himself?

I had invited my best friends in Sag Harbor, Dennis and Madeleine Hodgkins, who were also weekend residents and the owners of the two Labradors that are occasionally entrusted to my care. They, in turn, were bringing their own weekend guest, Jeremy Lipkin. We'd met once or twice before and I have to confess that I was already wondering if he and Renata could be a thing. That made eight.

Also on our esteemed list of invitees was John Hawes, an Englishman and prominent art dealer who had been living in New York for many years, and his current *inamorata*, another whom we had not yet met. John was also bringing with him a couple of graduate students from Columbia, both of whom were eager to meet Desi. That made twelve: the two of us, five friends, two friends of friends, a new girlfriend, and two complete unknowns. Even by our own standards, this was going to be interesting. But I loved the alchemy of it! Sometimes throwing these random elements together created magic. We would have to wait and see.

Renata was the first to arrive, and she looked absolutely terrific: tan, fit, nails aglow, beautifully dressed in a perfectly casual way, a small hamper of Manhattan delights hanging on one of her elbows.

'You didn't need to do this, Renata. Sag Harbor isn't the end of the universe.'

'Of course I didn't need to, but I have to keep my local delicatessen in business or the entire neighborhood will fall apart.'

'Think global, spend local. You *are* good.'

'It's harder and harder to do, you know. The franchises are everywhere on the East Side these days; it's tough for the little guy, but they seem to hang on.'

'Well, the franchises have made it into Sag Harbor and the Hamptons as well. But we can still get local fish and local poultry and even local wine.'

'Local wine? Does Desmond approve?' Renata couldn't resist a jibe.

'If it's good wine, sure; you know, Renata, he's not a snob about such things.' And there I went on the defensive again.

Note to *moi-même:* should I put that on my business card as well?

'And have you had some quality time together?'

'*Mais oui, ma chere!* He arrived yesterday afternoon. A bang-up beginning to the weekend.'

'Now you're talking, Abby, and I don't even need to pry into the details.'

'Good, because my native modesty would forbid me from replying,' I said, and we both laughed as our short commute brought us to the captain's door.

By one o'clock almost everyone had

assembled. After introducing Dolores, an exotically named and rather voluptuous redhead, John informed us that our two graduate students would arrive later, in time for dinner, and so we all sat down to lunch by the pool. Desi had chilled the rosé, sautéed some fresh spinach, and cooked several beautiful pieces of swordfish on the grill. I had made a salad of fennel, blood oranges, and thinly sliced red onion that I had soaked in lemon juice beforehand. And then there was homemade lemon, vanilla, and strawberry ice cream to finish us off — homemade, but just not made in my particular home.

We soon learned that David's friend, Richard Yung, a rather beautiful Chinese American, was a new research assistant in the Met's textiles department, specializing in Asian silks and other old fabrics. He and David obviously enjoyed each other's company very much, though David did let me know in passing that they weren't quite yet fully fledged partners. Would I need to double-check the sleeping arrangements? Probably not.

Renata instantly warmed to Jeremy, a good-looking, unassuming businessman with a passion, on the side it turned out, for jazz and New York's club scene. (I couldn't have planned it better if I'd tried.) Dennis and Madeleine, two of the most easy-going of my friends, were super-relaxed and chatty. I had met Dennis, an architect, while refurbishing my house; and Madeleine, who is a landscape designer, had been great with ideas for the garden. As a couple, they made for a nice package deal, as they like to say – a marriage made in design school, if not in heaven. All good.

The potential spark in this weekend tinderbox would, as usual, be the irrepressible John Hawes, who had already settled into his customary role of having an opinion on virtually every subject. From the kitchen, where I was absently stacking dishes, I could hear John make his verbal deliveries in that beautifully clipped accent. Desi had once pointed out that only Eton or Winchester or Harrow (Winchester in his case) could possibly produce anything like it. John's normal animation was only heightened, I sensed, by the addition of his new girlfriend, who was herself rarely at a loss for words. Dolores, we soon learned, had been a dancer, an actress, and a production assistant; she was now a scene designer, working both in the ballet and the theater. And she was quite theatrical herself, dressed with a cotton bandana tied around her ample breasts, a colorful cotton skirt, and spiked heels that had, I guaranteed, never seen a beach on Long Island before. The two of them made quite a couple, he holding forth whenever possible, she dramatically interrupting him whenever the conversation turned in her general direction.

Once lunch had been consumed and coffee served, it was time to see if everyone could be cajoled to take a short drive and spend some time at our favorite beach, *terra incognita* to those who don't know the South Fork fairly well. I quietly predicted to Desi that Dolores was likely to be a holdout, but much to my surprise she immediately agreed, changed into an equally colorful and exotic swimsuit, thereby making it quite clear to her pale Englishman that he had no choice but to slather on the sun-block and join her. We arranged the ten of us in three cars together with towels, magazines, cans of soda, bottles of water, and a hamper filled with fruit.

It really was a perfect afternoon: full sun, moderate heat, and mercifully bereft of the flies that call our beaches home throughout the summer months. As soon as everyone was settled, and having exchanged a quick glance at each other, Desi and I quietly made our way down the shoreline. I admired his tan and lean form, which was barely concealed by his black swimsuit – smallish but several styles more modest than the wonderfully skimpy things Richard and David were sporting. But that was Desi through and through. He took meticulous care of himself, but he chose not to flaunt it – not in public anyway. Renata and I, on the other hand, had chosen the thong and bikini-top option, a gesture that was certain to draw Jeremy's attention.

'Well, my Abby,' Desi said with a smile, 'how have you survived meal number one? Fairly raucous, I thought.'

'A little maybe, but fun. John is always outrageous — and don't get me wrong, I love him for that — but this Dolores seems to have placed him on steroids.'

'And probably Viagra as well. So prepare yourself for this evening, when we'll have no fewer than twelve intelligent New Yorkers ready to untether their hobbyhorses on each other.'

'Never fear, Dr. Fairbrother, I'm always prepared. Plan A: we start with drinks outside so that we can break into two or three groups.'

'Plan B,' Desi responded: 'we seat John and Dolores as far apart from each other as possible.'

'Plan C.' My turn again. 'If John takes over the conversation at the table, as doubtless he will at some point, I'll throw you a topic. Any ideas?'

'I always have ideas.' And then, softly dropping a few beachcombing treasures into my palm, he added, 'how about sea glass?'

'Sea glass, Desi? That's our lifeline?'

'Sea glass. There's quite a bit to say about it. Come on, old girl; help me collect some more.'

Well, it was hard for me to argue with that, and so we continued to collect our green and white (and occasional aqua) samples, worn beautifully smooth by months if not years of tidal ebb and flow. When the sun finally made the beginning of its late-summer nosedive, we turned and made our way back to our sand-spattered revelers, joining Jeremy and Renata for a leisurely swim. David and Richard had taken a long walk in the other direction, and the other two couples continued to secure the beachhead by reading, gossiping, and napping.

When it was almost five, I summoned everyone back to the cars so that we would have time to shower and change before our two final guests arrived. Deciding that it would make sense to learn a little more about them, I arranged for John and Dolores to drive with us back to Sag Harbor.

'So who exactly are these two characters you're going to foist upon us, John?' Desi asked from the front seat.

'I don't know them well but they seem like very nice young chaps. They're both at Columbia, finishing their dissertations. Andy Cameron and Jack Springer,' John added.

'Both in art history?' I asked.

'No. Jack is; he's writing a dissertation on portraiture and the novel during the Regency period in England. But Andy is in English literature, I believe, writing about the modern novel.'

'Then why is he interested in meeting me?'

'Because he's focusing on the role of the connoisseur in English and American fiction. You know, Henry James and the other usual suspects.'

'Thank God,' I cried, 'another book person. And here was I thinking I'd be completely surrounded by all of you art and design types.'

'How did you meet them?' Desi asked.

'I was invited, with a few other dealers, to participate in a seminar at Columbia this past spring. I met them there. When they learned that you and I were friends, they embarked on a relentless campaign to get me to introduce them to you. They've come along to the gallery for an opening and I've had them over to my apartment for drinks a couple of times But I've held out on you until now! Anyway, Desmond, they seem to be reasonably civilized — for graduate students, that is.' (John is notoriously wary of academics, no matter how young they are.)

'I hope you're right,' Desi teased.

'Just to warn you though. Andy, the chap in English literature, is a bit on the serious side. Probably gay, I'd guess.'

'Definitely gay,' Dolores interrupted.

Desi and I stole a furtive glance at each other.

'And Jack,' John continued, 'is a bit rough-edged; not quite what you would expect in a budding art historian. But he works hard, I gather, and seems to have his admirers. Nothing to worry about.'

'Tell me, Dolores,' I asked conspiratorially, 'is he attractive?'

'This Jack? Oh, yes, if you like the muscular

type, I suppose. Big jaw, broad shoulders, and who knows what else.

'But he's nothing compared to a middle-aged Englishman, right darling?' she added.

Ooh la la! I had to give her credit for that one. And I could just see, through my rearview mirror, our friend John flash his most brilliant smile — and wisely decline, for once, to make an answer.

Saturday, 16 September

When we arrived back at the house, I was surprised to see two young men sitting on my front steps, laughing together and waving as we pulled into the driveway. They were more than a little early — and I found myself having to give a regal welcome to them in a thong, a bandeau, and red-and-black flipflops. I can't deny that I was a touch annoyed at having to introduce them to Desi, who was almost as scantily attired as I was.

As it turned out, Jack and Andy were completed unfazed. They both seemed remarkably relaxed for advanced graduate students: more like schoolboys set out on an adventure. They had reached us, in fact, by taking a bus, hitchhiking, and walking, which suited them just fine. So after John and Dolores and everyone else had greeted them, I sent them to their rooms to change for a quick swim in the pool and lined everyone else up for indoor or outdoor shower duty. Dennis, Madeleine, and Jeremy escaped down the road, promising to return around seven.

This gave us a chance to get dinner on the road. A dinner that would unfold fairly smoothly. The key to such entertainments, I've learned, is to keep the meal simple, serve plenty of good drink, and invite the right people. No problem with the drink, I thought, and as for the guests — well, we would soon see. As for the dinner itself, Desi marinated butterflied legs of lamb for the grill and would produce a fragrant bowl of rice and a tureen of what he calls 'burnt carrots': 'just peel five pounds of them, serrate them in the food processer, and cook them down with butter, salt, and pepper for a couple of hours. About the most intensely tasting vegetable dish I know.'

My job was to produce a phalanx of light *hors d'oeuvres*, a large salad, and a second helping of ice cream, this time as an accompaniment to an ambitious trifle — if trifles can be called ambitious — that I had made with local apricots, plums, and berries. When we were done we went upstairs to shower in the master suite on the second floor. Desi had pulled on some beautiful yellow trousers, his much-loved espadrilles, and a white polo shirt on which I had had a local seamstress embroider Captain Logan's initials. His still damp dark blond hair made him look as fresh as a schoolboy, ready for his next adventure.

I had planned to wear a black skirt and (you guessed it) a red blouse, but the spectacle of Dolores earlier in the day spurred me on to something more louche. I knocked on Renata's door and asked if she wanted to join me in wearing nothing but a scarf on top.

'Show me what it looks like first, Abby.' This was my marvelously suspicious Renata. And so I quickly swung the heavy silk scarf around my neck and tied it in back, much to her approval.

'Very smart, Abby. And your short dark hair sets off those incredible shoulder blades of yours!'

'Paris or Rome?' I asked, thanking her with a smile and offering her a selection of seaside silks.

'I like the blue one with the white shovels and sand buckets on it. Parisian?'

'No, Roman. Or perhaps Ostian. I'll have to check.' I carefully wrapped the scarf around her torso and gave her a thumbs-up. 'You look fabulous, Renata. Just don't catch the knot on the back of your chair.'

'Forget it, Abby. After our duel-by-thong this afternoon, I don't think we've got too much more to hide.'

'And Jeremy?'

'Nice so far. Thanks for both raising and lowering the age limit for your old friend.'

I returned to our bedroom, changed out the black skirt for some silver-colored silk trousers, put on my highest Sag Harbor heels, and made my way downstairs to the kitchen. Desi was already at work and our guests, thank God, were still upstairs.

'Plan A?' I asked.

'Check.'

'Plan B?'

'Ditto.'

'Plan C?'

'I'm ready when you are, my dear Abigail.'

Okay, I thought. The next step was to collect our ten closest friends in the two front sitting rooms and ply them with cocktails and wine. Perhaps a bit less for John, come to think of it.

I brought in two wine chillers filled with ice and several bottles of sauvignon blanc — the French variety, which I much prefer to our native Californian, and even to what now comes to us from New Zealand. 'Kiwi cat pee,' Desi elegantly calls it, but he drinks it nonetheless.

But not tonight. The alternative to the white Bordeaux would be rum and tonic, one of Desi's favorites as long as the heat of summer is still upon us. *Canapés* on silver chargers. Candles and soft lighting. All rather different from our luncheon *al fresco* earlier in the afternoon.

As I fussed over the settings and eyeballed the flower arrangements again, I felt – how would John put it? – nicely chuffed by how successfully these two rooms work together. The problem, of course, is the small front hallway and large Queen Anne staircase that separate them. My solution, which his nibs actually approved, was to make them virtually identical: same paint, same sisal rug, same lighting, same grouping of sofas and chairs, and similar silver accessories around each room. The effect, I thought, was both crisp and relaxing. Creamy walls, slightly darker upholstery, a selection of pillows darker still, and very dark polished floors under the sisal rugs. Even the photographs hanging on the walls are by the same artist: striking images in black and white of rocks, sand, and sea, with the boundary between land and water blurred.

And nothing chintzy, slipcased, or needle-pointed in sight! These are comfortable rooms, but they are tightly tailored, and the fact that they are mirror images of each other pulls them psychologically together. If you're enjoying yourself in one room, you might just want to check on what's happening in that parallel universe across the hallway.

Almost precisely at seven our guests descended from the upper floors and returned from Dennis and Madeleine's house. Renata and I briefly basked in the success of our brave attire, but we were soon upstaged by Dolores's latest creation, a soft blazer with nothing beneath it save Dolores herself, shown to greatest advantage by a button placed rather lower than is commonly allowed.

Everyone else was dressed informally, which made our younger friends all the more comfortable. While we moved into the sitting rooms, Desi asked the two newcomers if they would please entertain him while he put his lamb on the grill and attended to his duties in the kitchen. By the time I checked on them ten minutes later, he had them both hard at work while he asked them questions about their scholarly interests.

While Andy and Jack turned the lamb again, Desi and I decided how to place our guests at the table. I was to have Andy on my left so that we could talk literature, while Jack's interest in portraiture persuaded Desi to keep him at his end of the table, next to Renata. We were rather short on women, but that hardly mattered. John would be on my right. Dolores would sit on Desi's right, and Jeremy, Richard, David, Dennis, and Madeleine would be seated on both sides near the center. The two major goals seemed to have been accomplished: Andy and Jack would receive special attention, and John and Dolores would be safely parted from each other. Plan B was complete.

As for plan A, that turned out to be the easiest part of all. Once the appetizers had vanished — along with several bottles of wine and a fair share of my best Jamaican grog — I seated everyone at the table and Desi poured the Graves, which had been breathing in various decanters for the last few hours.

'Before we begin,' I told our guests, 'I'd like

to ask you to join me in a simple ritual. When we have groups of friends together, and that includes new friends as well as old, we like to go around the table before we eat. It's not grace exactly, but you each have to say something that you're thankful for — beyond, of course, the fact that you're here with us in Sag Harbor and about to tuck into Desmond's lamb and claret. Renata, you're an old hand at this, why don't you go first?'

Renata, with nary a hesitation: 'A beautiful day, lovely friends, Abby,' and then, smiling at Jeremy, 'and a nice friend of lovely friends.'

Moi: 'Well put, old friend. Okay, Jack, your turn.'

'Meeting both of you, of course,' he said, with more than a bit of sycophancy, I thought. 'And, well, seeing how the other half lives.'

'Well, at least you're honest about it, Jack,' Desi grinned. 'And some day you, too, will have a decent job. Next year, let's hope. Madeleine?'

'Having a friend who likes Labradors — and doesn't mind hosting them in the kitchen or the pool.'

I blew Madeleine a little kiss, but was imagining what I might do if one of the dogs ever so much as set foot in one of my lovely sitting rooms.

'Sweet! How about you, David?'

'Working at the Met, working at the Met,

working at the Met. And meeting Richard there, of course, as well.'

'Nice to know that you don't have an entirely one-track mind, David,' Desi added, pleased to see David learning to relax a little in company.

I was pleased, too. Such a lovely young man, and so bright a future unless he worked himself to death!

All eyes moved to John, who in a voice quivering with would-be, just-might-be sentimentality opined: 'The few remaining men of taste in this country, among whom I count you, of course, dear Desmond.' Baleful sounds in all directions. 'And the new lease my little gallery has been enjoying. And what lies just beneath the surface of Dolores's seductive jacket.'

'Oh please, darling; you're absolutely incorrigible,' Dolores beamed, sucking up the attention with glee while winking at me and Renata.

'And he'll probably be even worse later on, so be warned.' I passed the hypothetical baton onto Andy – the hostess's prerogative.

'Not to embarrass you, Abby, but being able to talk about fiction with someone who actually writes it. That's not how it usually works in graduate school.'

'Thank you, Andy. Impossible to embarrass, easy to flatter – that's me. Where do you young people learn your manners these days? Not in the dives we hung out in back then, eh Renata?' I noticed her sideways glance at Andy. Not completely comfortable, my complicated Renata, but she brightened up with Jeremy's quip: 'Continuing surges in the financial markets. No, just kidding!'

'Now wait a second, Jeremy,' John interjected. 'That's not such a bad idea. A high tide raises all boats, including those in the art world.'

'And you might just add, John, that an ebbing tide *also* raises boats in the art world,' Desi sagely added. 'Just think of all those hard-pressed collectors who suddenly find that they have to deaccession their expensive purchases.'

'So true, Desmond, so true. We anticipate our commissions on the downward slope as well.'

'Like birds of prey?'

This took everyone by surprise, especially as it came from young Jack Springer, who seemed not to be a bit perturbed by his own impetuousness.

'Exactly: birds of prey!' Dolores helpfully added. 'But in sweet John's case, a hawk rather than a vulture.'

'Thank you, sweetheart. I may be an old bird, but I still have a few new tricks to play — even on the downward slope.'

'Richard, I think it's your turn.' I'd noticed a certain reluctance to join in with this particular banter, but then, we were all new to him.

'Like David, I'm delighted to be in New York.' He flushed a little but continued. 'I've lived in San Francisco almost my entire life, and although I love it when I return, it seems rather small after New York — and perhaps a little parochial.'

'It *is* small and parochial, but then almost anywhere that isn't New York is as well, even London.'

'Thank you, John; of course Richard's sentiments would have carried no weight without your approval.' It was all playful, of course, but much as John was good value, he could be a little intimidating when you didn't know him. Even I felt protective towards David's fine-boned, ethereal friend. 'Now, what about Dennis?'

'Abby, I'm grateful that you've restored this lovely old house with such affection and tact. I'm entranced every time I sit here at the table with you.'

'Thanks, sweetie. Well you know that I've always had a soft spot for ridiculous wallpaper, but I actually think that I've been quite restrained with my *Toile de Jouy*.'

'*Toile* forever!' Dennis applauded enthusiastically.

'Amen.'

'My turn?' Dolores was clearly bursting to speak. 'Well, I'm absolutely delighted to be *out* of the city that Richard and David have been extolling. We're only two weeks past Labor Day and the pace is already too much! This is such a charming place you have here, Abby —'

'– and where else can my beautiful friend wear three outfits in the same day?' John threw Dolores his own kiss.

'Well, on that note perhaps I should add that I'm thankful tonight for thongs and scarves and' (looking down the table at John) 'red socks and seersucker as well, of course. And, just a shade more seriously,' Desi continued, 'I'm thankful to see that there's a younger generation of humanists at the table this evening; the future belongs to you.'

'Yet be it less or more, or soon or slow,
It shall be still in strictest measure ev'n
To that same lot, however mean or high,
Toward which Time leads me, and the will of
  Heav'n.'

I knew how to do a party piece when I wanted to, and I secretly enjoyed the stunned silence that followed, interrupted a few seconds later by Desi.

'My God, Abby. Do you have poetic tags for everyone else at the table?'

'No, Desmond; only for you.'

'Was it Keats, my dear?'

'Too heavenly for Keats, I'm afraid.'

'Milton, one of the early sonnets, no?' Andy didn't waste a second in displaying his reputation as a literary scholar.

'You're absolutely right, Andy. And with that I

thank the heavens for the forces that have brought us all together — and I officially pronounce this the end of general conversation. Be nice to your dinner partners, and let us know if you'd like seconds.'

It was time for me to be nice to Andy and John, but first I cast a long glance down the table at Desi, who gave me a barely discernible wink. Plan A was underway, Plan B was in effect, and Plan C lay nicely in abeyance. So far, so good — and the lamb and carrots and claret were rather better than good.

As we moved on to dessert about forty-five minutes later, I realized that I had been lax in my vigilance, however. Having talked at some length with John — about his gallery, the fall auctions, the collectors he was carefully nurturing – I had turned to Andy for a little too long, leaving the group at large at the mercy of John. This was a major no-no and something I had been charged with preventing. I realized that it was time for me to throw a certain life-line down the table.

'I'm sorry, John; I hate to interrupt. But does anyone around the table know anything about sea glass?'

'Sea glass?' John retorted, his flushed face setting off his white hair even more dramatically than usual. 'What about it?' The interruption had the desired effect of stopping John in his tracks for a moment.

'I, for one, am interested in it from the point of view of being a collector,' Desi said. 'I wonder whether, from your point of view, John, you see as many collectors as you used to when you first started out. Is there a new generation of collectors constantly being born?'

John paused several seconds before responding. 'You've in fact asked several questions, Desmond. There are, to be sure, more people buying works of art than ever before — partly, I suppose, because there are more people on this planet than ever before! But are they really collectors? Not always. Some are fairly savvy investors, some are decorators, and some just seem to be testing the waters. But there still are collectors, of course: knowledgeable, passionate, keenly focused. They're what make my own work so gratifying.'

'Are they constantly coming along?' Desi asked.

'Slowly. I have a few younger clients, but they're the exception. Normally one has to reach a certain level of financial comfort as well as have the leisure time to devote to it. My perfect client is a successful man in his mid-fifties who doesn't play golf or own a 30-foot ketch.'

'Married?'

'Ideally not. But if so, attached to an incredibly understanding wife with money of her own.'

'Might she be a collector herself?'

Here it was: cat and mouse, Desi's favorite game. But where, precisely, was our professor *emeritus* headed? And when would John stand down?

'Female collectors tend to act on their own, whether or not they are married,' John answered. 'I know of very few couples who collect together — and not necessarily with great distinction. It's a bit like having a committee make a decision for you: always a bit of a compromise.'

'Do you know of any couples who collect *against* each other?' Desi continued.

John paused once again, but only briefly. 'I can't think of any, but I did once know a very serious book collector who specialized in children's literature. He was a diplomat who collected books by the armful wherever he was posted. He confided to me one evening that he had amassed one of the largest collections of children's books in private hands. I asked him if he had any serious rivals, and you won't believe his answer: "Just one," he said; "my sister."'

John had everyone laughing, but Desi was unrelenting.

'Sibling rivalry with a vengeance, John; too good to be true! But your story raises another question, doesn't it. They may always have been rivals, but were your friend and his sister always collectors?'

'Well, Desmond, I've always assumed that they fought over their books when they were children and just never gave it up.'

'Possibly, John, but you're really sidestepping my question. Were they born collectors, or did they attach themselves to their books as a form of compensation?'

'Compensation for what?' John asked.

'Compensation for parental neglect, or parental preference for the other child, or for some other form of anxiety or deficiency.'

'I don't think that I can answer that, Desmond; I didn't really know my diplomatic friend that well.'

'But I'm not really asking about your friend, John. Let me phrase my question slightly differently. Aren't you fond of saying that one is either a collector or one isn't?'

'Yes, I plead guilty to saying that. And I do believe it.'

'Do you consider yourself to be a collector?'

'I do — but dealers are rather special collectors on the whole. We may buy something for our own collection, but if the price is high enough, we sometimes deaccession items as well,' John concluded.

'Ah yes,' Desi quickly added, 'that downward slope we were talking about earlier. I guess it's comforting to know that even dealers are not immune to common economic factors.

'But if I hear you correctly, John,' he continued, 'there are collectors — and then there are collectors. You already seem to have a crack in your airtight proposition. Let's see if there are others.'

Desi then looked around the room and asked each of us if we were collectors.

'Andy?'

'I never met a book I didn't like, but I don't buy them in any organized fashion. If it's something that looks interesting, I usually buy it. And if you're a graduate student, books do furnish a room.'

'Well put, Anthony Powell. What about you, Richard?'

'Not yet. Perhaps when I'm in my mid-fifties.'

'And you, Jack? If you can't afford to collect now, would you like to do so later on? Perhaps a small collection of Regency portraits?'

'If they're any good, I think that such paintings deserve to be in the public domain rather than owned by private collectors.'

'Fair enough. But you evaded my question.'

'No, I don't think of myself as a collector.'

'And you, David?'

'Desmond, you know that I collect, and probably always have. Coins, then stamps, then prints and the occasional drawing. It's a pretty modest collection, but I love the pursuit, and the odd discovery, and then the challenge of arranging it all.'

'Walter Benjamin could not have put it more succinctly, David,' Desi added. At the mere mention of Benjamin, a rustle of excitement arose among the twenty-somethings.

'Desmond,' Jack said, 'I thought that, as a Marxist, Benjamin was a critic of the "aura" that attaches itself to original works of art — that he was a celebrant of the age of mechanical reproduction.'

'You're right, Jack, but people (even good Marxists) are complicated beings. Benjamin was also a very serious collector, and he wrote a lovely essay on unpacking his library and placing it on his shelves. He was particularly interested in that moment when an object leaves the realm of the ordinary — of everyday utility — and crosses a threshold into the realm of the collected. There's a wonderful passage, in fact, where he writes about objects being released from what he called the "bondage of being useful."'

'But isn't collecting,' Richard asked, 'just another form of bondage? I'm thinking of all of those connoisseurs who keep their treasures entirely to themselves.'

'And I'm wondering, Desmond,' Dennis added, 'whether all objects actually change their nature once they're collected. As an architect, I'm particularly interested in how my clients' furniture fits into the design of the house itself. When I select a chair for them — or for Madeleine and myself, for that matter — I suppose that I'm collecting it, but I'm also putting it to use.'

'Unless you put it in a museum,' Dolores added, 'with a velvet cord in front of it and a "Don't Sit Here" sign placed on its seat.'

'And isn't it also true, Desmond,' Madeleine asked, 'that some objects really never have utilitarian uses in the first place? Is a painting a utilitarian object?'

'That depends on the painting, I'd say,' David answered.

'Which brings us to sea glass,' Desi announced.

Bemused silence once again around the table.

'It clearly has no practical purpose,' Desi said. 'It simply washes up on our beaches. And yet some of us — perhaps not too many of us — pick it up when we see it in the sand. Does that make us collectors?'

'Doesn't it depend on whether we keep the pieces or not?' I asked.

'And what we do with them when we take them home?' Dolores added.

'Fair enough,' Desi continued. 'Let's assume that we keep them and that we place them with other pieces of sea glass: green with green, aqua with aqua, blue with blue, and so forth. Does that make us collectors?'

'Not in my book.' This, of course, was John's

response. 'Collecting is not the same thing as hoarding, nor is it the same thing as choosing one brand of toothpaste rather than another. True collecting is based on the preservation of cultural objects, either privately or for an institution. Everything else is mere dabbling.'

'So we seem,' Desi continued, 'to have a continuum but not a consensus. At one end of the spectrum everyone is a collector, in the sense that we all make decisions each day about choosing one thing rather than another. And at the other end we have John's focused, disciplined, passionate collector of paintings and rare books and American highboys, even approaching the realm of obsessive or pathological behavior in certain cases. How do we adjudicate such a wide divide?'

'Perhaps one way would be to place less attention on *what* is collected and more attention on what the act of collecting signifies in the life of the collector. Isn't this whole business about collecting based on motivation and behavior?' This interesting proposal came from Jeremy, who had been silent during the discussion so far.

'But there's still a major difference between sea glass and a nineteenth-century photographic seascape, isn't there?' Richard asked. John, of course, nodded in approval.

'Not to the person who is obsessed with collecting sea glass,' I answered. 'And the same would surely hold true for anyone else who collects objects from the natural world. Fossils, seashells, butterflies.'

'Does sea glass come from the natural world?' Desi asked the table at large. 'How does it get into the water and onto our beaches in the first place?'

Jack: 'It comes from glass bottles, of course.'

Madeleine: 'Which are made by humans — and which are disposed of by humans.'

'Ah, Desmond, I think I see what you're getting at,' David added. Clearly the light bulb had finally flashed on. 'Glass is made by humans, but it's made from sand. So human activity produces an artificial product from the natural world. Then we, as humans, discard some of these bottles back into the sea, where the sand acts not as the base material but as the agent that produces the final, beautifully sculpted object. Which we, as humans, pick up, decide to discard or keep, and then preserve in our collections — or, I imagine, turn into jewelry or some other collectible.'

'You don't have to imagine, David,' I interposed. 'Desmond has actually had some lovely earrings made for me from the sea glass we've harvested.'

'So, Desmond, I think I see what you've been up to,' Andy concluded. 'You've used a fairly humble example of what *might* be collected in order to make us all fine-tune our own notions of what it means to collect. And yet your humble example turns out to be fairly complicated once we consider the process by which it comes into being, involving both natural and artificial processes.'

'Nicely put, both of you, worthy of any seminar I used to lead,' Desi said. 'And now you can stay up as late as you want arguing with John, but dinner — including Abby's wonderful dessert — is now officially over.'

'There's more wine in the kitchen, port in the pantry, and water in the pool,' I added. 'We'll see you in the morning. And thank you, Renata, for snapping pictures of all of us during Dr. Fairbrother's latest symposium.'

And with that we cleared the table, kissed and hugged our guests, and beat a graceful retreat to the second floor as soon as it was polite to do so.

'Well, my love,' I remarked as soon as I could corner him, 'you certainly know what to do when a lifeline is thrown in your direction. You clever thing: you made John the center of attention but worked it so that he barely got a word in edgewise. I must hand it to you.'

'Thank you, Miss Higginson. All in a night's work. And leave it to David and Andy to piece it all together: very nicely done, although I thought that David seemed rather quiet. I hope everything's all right with him. And we certainly detected more than a little attitude in young master Springer.'

'More than you suspect.'

'Do tell.'

'While you were chatting with the other youngsters, Jack propositioned me at the kitchen sink.'

'Did he really? My word. And in such a romantic setting — and with the putative master of the house only a few yards away!'

'I was certainly surprised, to say the least, but I couldn't help but be a little flattered.'

'I wonder whether it was your thong or your dessert that prompted such a move. And how did you respond, may I ask?'

'Not here, not now.'

'Good girl. I have my own plans for you this evening.'

'And what might *they* be?!'

'Just wrap those lovely legs of yours around my neck and you'll see.'

'*Avec les talons – ou sans?*'

'With your heels on, of course!'

And so — at last — to bed.

Wednesday, 19 September

I can't honestly say that I led Desi kicking and screaming to my architectural soirée the following Wednesday. Let's just say that he arrived downtown with more skepticism than enthusiasm — and I can't entirely blame him. This wasn't really any more *my* scene than it was his, but a job is a job, and he understood that I needed these commissions to keep body and soul together. Having promised to do it, I needed to see the premises in full swing before I could decide how to write my tart little essay and suggest exactly the right photographs to my editor. Renata, who had become more enamored of her new camera with every day that passed, had agreed to serve as my unofficial photographer (the magazine would arrange for its own shoot a few days later). That made us three for one and one for all until Renata announced that she had invited Jeremy Lipkin as well, which brought us to full complement. I very much doubted that we would bump into any of our other friends at this rather odd event.

I had tried to set the scene for Desi and Renata as carefully as possible, hoping that a little knowledge would allay their misgivings. Whether I had been successful or not, it was hard to say.

Sometimes a little knowledge is a dangerous thing, as my favorite literary hunchback once pontificated. Actually, I think that a little knowledge is *always* a dangerous thing — but then, as a novelist, I suppose that a little knowledge is what I usually have to work with.

Here's how I pitched it to Desi. 'So it's like this: people visit your Carriage House and the thing they notice is the contrast between what they see as a modern building with all the older paintings and antique furniture. So the place we're going to is just the other way around. The building is down in "High Chelsea" — and the building is as traditional as can be. High, ornamental ceilings. A good deal of first-rate molding on the walls. Dark oak floors. Fabulous chimneys and doors. Beautiful built-in shelving in the library. You get the picture, *mi amigo*. Looks as if it had been built on Park Avenue or Fifth before the first world war, whereas it was actually built even earlier than that — and then painstakingly renovated a few years ago.'

'This sounds rather promising, actually. How bad is the art?'

'I'm not the expert; I'll let you make your

own judgment. The *frisson*, as I understand it, is supposed to be produced by the juxtaposition of the old and the new, not the good and the bad.

Although that may prove to be the case as well!'

'Abby, I'm happy to join you, but with the usual proviso.'

'Aye, aye, captain: I know quite well how to jump ship with the best of them.'

'So you do — and it's never done you any harm.'

Here's how I pitched it to Renata. 'By all means, do invite Jeremy. It sounds like fun. And I'll be surprised if you don't meet a host of other eligible men in their thirties and forties as well.'

Which provoked the usual response: 'I'm not so sure, Abby. I've never put much faith in so-called win-win situations. Especially with men.'

Fair enough, old friend — although I don't exactly believe in the lose-lose category either.

We agreed to meet downtown at around seven, Desi and I in one cab, Renata and Jeremy in another. With a bow in the direction of this evening's clientele, Desi was wearing a midnight-blue suit — 'darker than black in artificial light, you know' — and a deep red tie with a suitably abstract design. 'Leave it to the French,' he said when I complimented him on said cravat.

I thought we might be fashionably early, but the place was already a madhouse when we arrived, with a waiting line in the hallway before one could penetrate the apartment's double front doors. Desi rolled those baby browns of his, but I quickly told him to buck up: worse was still to come.

'Explain to me again, darling, exactly what kind of event we're attending — if, indeed, we are lucky enough to be invited inside,' he asked.

'It's a public-relations event, the kind of thing that Renata sometimes devises. The couple in question — '

'Who are they again?' he asked.

'Ronald and Patricia Simmons. He's made some money on Wall Street and decided to invest in contemporary art.'

'What do you mean by "invest"? Is he holding or selling?'

'He's selling. The concept is supposed to be as novel as the juxtaposition of the art and the apartment. Instead of opening a gallery, he's actually opening up his home. If you like something, you can call him up for a return visit.'

'Ah yes, I know the set-up: he gives you a glass of white wine and you present him with a six-figure check. I can only imagine what our friend John Hawes would make of this!'

'Who knows, Desi; John might actually learn something from such an occasion.'

At this point we were suddenly buoyed into the apartment in a gentle surge and promptly handed tall flutes of very good champagne.

Although I had studied photographs of the Simmons's home in various stages of renovation, I wasn't actually prepared for what confronted us. Even with a surfeit of sleek, well-groomed New Yorkers within it, the place was quite overpowering. The doors, walls, windows, columns, and cornices were all painted rich shades of cream, and the entire entrance hallway absolutely glowed.

There were no rugs on the floors, which were stained a dark coffee color and had a high, fine sheen to them. The lamps that hung from the fourteen-foot ceiling above us were essentially large sculptural objects — sparkling cubes made of plastic and crystal. I wondered whether *they* were for sale as well.

There was only one large geometrical painting hanging in the entryway; for a proper view of the owners' collection, we had to make our way to the front sitting room, which turned out to be an enormous gallery almost forty feet long. Even Desmond Fairbrother seemed to be impressed.

'Well, Abby,' he whispered, 'this is certainly a *piano nobile* — although it lacks, of course, both a piano and the nobility, unless Wall Street barons still count among our local aristocracy.'

'Of course they do. Think of the Simmonses as

a baronet and his lady: a good name, some hereditary money, and even more money generated downtown. Are you ready to meet them?'

'Not yet. Let's explore a bit more and focus on the art.'

Exploring wasn't actually that easy, given the number of people and the climbing decibel levels. The library, thank God, had real books in it, although the artistic motif was sculptural: twisted and tormented figures of humans and animals, some small enough to be showcased in the bookshelves, some large enough to dominate their respective corners. It was not a room in which I, for one, would feel comfortable curled up with a good book, but it had its own integrity and the volumes on the shelves were rather impressive. Not just the usual oversized tomes devoted to modern art and architecture, but also old-master *catalogues raisonnés*, auction catalogues, long runs of the leading magazines, what looked to be a complete set of the Library of America, shorter runs of the Pleiades editions and the Loeb classics, and even a small but interesting section devoted to the history of collecting. It was, in short, a working library, furnished — as were all of the other rooms — with handsome pieces of furniture in a variety of creamy textures.

'Must be the new taupe,' Desi quipped.

'You're just jealous,' I responded.

'Desmond jealous! I can't imagine that, Abby.' Renata gave us both a hug and Jeremy bestowed a friendly kiss. 'Sorry we're late,' she added. 'We had to go through a complete passport and visa check on the way in, but at least the champagne is worth the ticket of admission.'

'And what do you think of this as an event, Renata? Successful from your professional point of view?' I asked.

'Of course it is. Any event is successful if you have to wait in line and then can't breathe once you enter. What more could you ask for?'

'And you, Jeremy; what do you make of this cultural mayhem?' I asked.

'I think it's really par for the course, to be honest with you. My successful friends are doing much the same thing, although perhaps not on this scale — and perhaps not to sell what they've been collecting. With these lavish Wall Street bonuses, what are you going to do once you've invested them in a second or third house, a boat and a Bentley, and 529s for your kids and grandchildren? The answer is art, and the people I know are more comfortable with what is new and fresh and hasn't got a lot of professional opinion attached to it already.'

'And the challenge,' Desi said, 'is for people like John Hawes and myself to persuade some of these very intelligent people to look backwards as well as forwards from time to time. But why must most of the art be contemporary?'

'And so edgy,' Renata added. 'I don't think that I could live with anything we've seen so far.'

'I don't mind the edge,' Desi responded. 'All good art should stimulate us to see the world in a new way. And the fact that some paintings were executed in Europe in the seventeenth or eighteenth century doesn't necessarily mean that they've been scrutinized to death. One could easily build a collection of French pastels or British watercolors that would be as fresh as anything produced today.'

'You mean *you* could build such a collection,' I corrected him.

'I think that anyone who could amass this collection should be capable of collecting at a much more sophisticated level.'

'At least there's nothing by Jeff Koons here,' I added.

'Or Hirst, or Schnabel. And that,' Desi added, 'is where we do have to give our collectors their due. So far as I can tell, virtually all of the artists represented here are unknown. That's a healthy sign of independence.'

By this time we had made our way through the dining room and two of the bedrooms, all of which were decorated in a similar clash of gutsy pictures and statues against the serene backdrop of creamy paints and fabrics. As we entered a third bedroom — which, judging by its size, must be the master suite — we found our hosts enjoying a quiet moment on a loveseat placed at the foot of the bed. They seemed to be enjoying the evening as well as the champagne they were serving. I got ready to introduce myself.

'Good evening, Patricia and Ronald,' I said, 'I'm Abigail Higginson. I'm writing an article about your wonderful apartment.'

'Oh yes,' Ronald Simmons answered, rising quickly from his seat. 'You're the novelist. I hope you like what you've seen so far.'

Patricia rose as well. They were both friendly, both forty-something, both attired in crisply tailored Italian suits — he in gray, she in black. They were a handsome couple, to say the least.

As we made all of our introductions, Patricia smiled at Desi and said, 'I'm sure you don't remember me, but I took one of your courses when you still taught at the Institute. I was Patricia Smith at the time.'

Desi looked at her for a moment and then said, 'I certainly remember your face. Which course did you take? It must have been either "Portraiture" or "The History of the Modern Print," I imagine.'

'It was portraiture, but quite a few years ago.'

Desi smiled at her and then, looking around the room, playfully suggested that his course on European portraiture didn't seem to have had much effect on her.

'Oh no,' she responded, 'that's where you're wrong. Why don't you all come with me.'

She quickly led us to another room that was part of the suite — a dressing room just as calmly turned out as all of the other rooms in the apartment, and boasting just one work of art on its walls. There, hanging above an identical cream-colored loveseat, was a sumptuous portrait of a young woman sitting at her spinet. She was beautifully, intricately painted, caught in a moment of reverie while playing her handsomely decorated instrument.

Patricia said nothing, and neither did we until Desi finally broke the spell. 'It's lovely, Patricia. I don't think that I've seen it before, but it certainly looks like a very good Vigée Le Brun, probably dating from the 1780s, near the end of the *ancien régime*. How long have you had it?'

'I bought it a few years ago, just as Ronald began to take an interest in contemporary art. I certainly trust that it *is* a Vigée Le Brun because I paid for it accordingly.' And then, with perfect timing, she added: 'And no matter what Ronald here may tell you, it's absolutely not for sale!'

'Nor should it be,' Desi said. 'It's perfect where it is, and perfect that it's yours.'

'Not bad for a graduate student, Dr. Fairbrother,' I chimed in.

'A recovering graduate student,' Patricia responded. 'I'm afraid that I didn't write a dissertation, but I enjoyed my years at the Institute immensely, and I hope that I've been able to draw on my experience there from time to time.'

'So you clearly have,' Desi added. 'And to be honest with you, I can't think of any higher compliment a teacher could enjoy than seeing this wonderful painting hanging in your boudoir. Is this something that Abby can include in her article, or do you wish to keep it private?'

'That's a difficult question. Perhaps,' she said, turning to me, 'we could have lunch together and talk it over.'

'You've got a deal,' I said. 'I'll make a reservation where no one will ever have heard of the *ancien régime*, believe me.'

Having paid our more-than-polite respects to our host and hostess in her sanctum sanctorum, we made our way to a champagne tray once again and then decided on our next move. Although the crowding had been intense, we had not bumped into anyone we knew — which certainly set a record. Desi invited us to have dinner at his club, but I could tell from the look on Renata's face that she had other plans in mind.

'That's a lovely idea, Desmond,' I intervened, 'but let's not make four a crowd if Jeremy and Renata have something else they'd like to do.'

'Actually,' Renata responded, 'I thought that I might show Jeremy a little of *my* New York this evening — someplace he's never been to and, with luck, has never heard of.'

'Desmond, we appreciate your invitation,' Jeremy added, 'but Renata is hard to resist. She may even take me to Coney Island or to the Bronx. Who knows?'

Fifteen minutes later Desi and I were nicely ensconced in the overstuffed chairs at his wonderful little club just off Park. I'm not a club kind of person, to say the least; I've seen enough of that in New England. But Desi's club — the only one he belongs to — is another story. Its collection of paintings and antique furniture is entirely British, and its members relish the understated good taste of their small, comfortable haven. 'Not even in London,' Desi likes to say, 'can you find a club named after a poem by Tennyson!'

After our drinks had arrived, I arched my eyebrows at my one-time professorial friend and asked him how well he remembered Patricia Simmons, neé Smith. 'I take it from her appearance tonight that she wasn't your standard-issue graduate student dressed in jeans, boots, granny glasses, and serious attitude.'

'You're right, Abby. She was elegant even then, over ten years ago, and I remember her as being well-trained before she arrived at the Institute, perhaps at Wellesley or Bryn Mawr.

'But she was fairly quiet back then,' he

continued. 'I certainly couldn't have envisioned her as a partner-in-crime when it came to building a major collection of contemporary art — let alone dealing in it. But that's the nice thing about people, they are actually capable of change, even if most of us ardently resist it. And the nice thing about Patricia, I must say, is that she bought a very beautiful, very expensive painting that will always remind her of the person she has also been.' And then, as an afterthought, 'I wonder where and when she found it? I certainly would have purchased it if I had had the wherewithal at the time.'

'And so, *caro mio*, were the two of you romantically involved?'

'Absolutely not. You need to remember that I never slept with my students during my years as a teacher. It may be fashionable, but I don't like the built-in disparity in such relationships. The temptation to abuse one's power — or to disregard the trust a student places in you — can be very strong.'

'That didn't stop you with me.'

'That was different, Abby. I was serving as a teaching fellow, aiding and abetting rather than judging your performance from on high. Just think of all the free tuition that came your way.'

'Free tuition? That's one way of putting it!'

'So let's just agree that we were both teaching each other a few tricks?'

'Agreed,' I said. 'And we still have a few more up our sleeves, don't you think?'

'Yes — but I can only speak for myself, of course.'

'Just think,' I said, 'of all the Yankee manners and mores you still don't completely understand.'

'Only a Yankee would talk about "mores." They don't seem to exist anywhere else.

'Only in your Bostonian orbit of Cabots and Lowells and Lorings, to say nothing of the infamous three P's.'

'What three P's?'

'Come on, Abby. How many friends or cousins or aunts do you have named Prudence, Patience, or Priscilla?'

'Is this your revenge for my having taken you to a certifiably glamorous event?'

'I'm waiting, Abby. Ten? Fifteen? Twenty?'

'Probably fifteen or so.'

'You know, I have a good friend in Chicago named Priscilla. She's a kind person, smart, quite beautiful. She got all the right degrees and she's been extremely successful as a lawyer — and no one, absolutely no one, calls her Priscilla. Nor would she allow them to.'

'So what does she call herself?' I asked.

'Pam.'

'Oh dear, Desi. Isn't that rather drab?'

'Not once you've met her, it isn't.'

'But there's something to be said for keeping

these old names alive, don't you think? We need our Jareds and Josiahs and Jedediahs, I think.'

'You may, but I don't. That's what so often rubbed this Midwesterner the wrong way in Cambridge and Boston: there are too many people there who seem to have no idea where they're headed, but are totally fixated on where they came from.'

'Fair enough, Desi; we could easily fill your house with them — '

'God forbid!' he replied. 'I have enough trouble with my own friends. That's why I enjoyed our time in Sag Harbor with our four young men: no baggage there, just real energy to get on with their lives, especially that Jack Springer.'

'But here's the other side of the coin. For every Bostonian obsessed with their roots, there are a dozen who know both where they're from and where they're headed. What I like most about my father and his closest friends is that their generosity has such wonderful historical roots. They're not philanthropic simply because it's expected of them. They do it because they believe in changing things for the better – as did their ancestors.'

'Yes, Abby, but your family and their friends are surely exceptions. No symphony without old what's-his-name, if I remember correctly.'

'You do. But they're not exceptions, Desi. I

could introduce you to dozens of people just like them.'

'Ah, yes: each with a seat at symphony, a share at the Athenæum, a plot at Mount Auburn — '

'And a close relative at McLean's,' I quickly added. 'The Bellevue of the north.'

'All right,' he replied, 'let's impose an official time-out on both of us. Let's debate dinner instead. Shall we order something here and then finish off the evening with dessert at my place?'

'That sounds like a plan,' I said. 'And you were a darling this evening, you know. Thanks for joining me. You do look particularly nice in midnight blue.'

'It does me good to get out, my dear, especially when our cutting-edge hostess confesses that she has a ravishing Vigée Le Brun in her boudoir.'

'Ravishing,' I mused. 'I wonder whether that comes before or after dessert?'

Thursday, 20 September

'Jesus Christ, Abby, what are you going to do?'

This was Renata, enjoying the lunch I was giving her the following day. A brief lunch, on the run, was the best we could do — but we did it well at a little trattoria we both adore in mid-town.

I hadn't checked my cell-phone for messages the previous evening. I tend not to, especially if I'm with Desi, who resorts to such devices only when he's traveling. So I didn't catch up with my little tele-prompter until I turned the phone on again that morning. It was the usual list of suspects — my mother in Boston, two girlfriends, my magazine editor — but then came an intriguing surprise. Jack Springer, our not-very-shrinking-violet of a graduate student, had left a polite message asking if I'd like to have a drink with him. And thus Renata's slightly bemused question.

'I'm going to see him,' I said, as calmly as I could. 'And why not? He's attractive, he's

94

intelligent, and he's persistent. Why not give him a little air time?'

'Air time! What the fuck does that mean?'

'Just what you think it means,' I answered. 'I should see what he has in mind.'

'What he has in mind?' she responded. 'I would be very surprised if he didn't have one specific thing in mind.'

'And what,' I thought aloud, 'would be wrong with that?'

This brought us to dessert, at which point we took our usual never-too-rich and never-too-thin pass on the *gelati* and *tiramisu* and ordered double espressos instead. And a piece of chocolate — a very, very small piece of chocolate — to sweeten our virtuous choice.

'I hope you know what you're doing,' she said.

'To be honest with you, Renata, I *don't* know exactly what I'm doing — and that's what makes it interesting. And exciting.'

'Well, he's certainly got nerve, I have to give him that. Cocky boy!'

'Just how cocky we'll soon see.'

I could feel the now familiar discomfort, a slight tension in the muscles of my cheek, a gentle clenching of the teeth, and knew it was time to change the focus. I love to shock Renata sometimes with what she seems to consider my flagrant promiscuity, mainly because her reaction is always amusing. But it was becoming harder to kid myself that these occasional conquests were as much fun as they used to be. I knew what I really wanted, just not whether I could have it.

'In the meantime I haven't heard boo from you about Jeremy. Where did you take him last night?'

'I decided to surprise him right here in Manhattan. There's a small hamburger joint hidden away in one of the nicer hotels on the West Side. You almost couldn't find it if someone didn't take you there. It's the real thing, with wooden booths and a jukebox and more than a little grease perfuming the air.'

'And what did Jeremy think?'

'He pretended to be charmed while we waited for our orders to arrive, and then — thank God — he capitulated the minute our burgers and fries showed up. I can't say that the wine list did the dinner justice, but we made up for that later at a rather nice bar in another part of the lobby.'

'Some lobby! And what then?'

'Hey, Abby, we're not quite at my-place-or-yours yet. I'm taking it one step at a time with him. And I must say that he's really a very easy going guy: no push, no shove. I feel comfortable with him, and I think that he respects the pace I'm setting.'

'And what comes next?'

'We'll do something this weekend, but it's still TBD. Got any ideas?'

'Well, you're welcome to use the house in Sag Harbor at some point, but right now I think I would suggest one of those five-borough bicycle rides. Are you up to it?'

'Of course I am,' she said. 'And you and Desmond?'

'Also TBD, although we may head out to the Island again, depending on the weather. Let's stay in touch.'

When I returned to my apartment, I spent most of the afternoon working on my essay for the shelter magazine. I knocked off work around six, took a long shower, and then contemplated my wardrobe for the evening. The weather was still warm — and I was still quite tanned — so I chose a lightweight black dress cut above the knee, tied a red-and-black scarf around my waist, and stepped into black shoes with long red heels. If I've learned anything from his Highness about clothing, it's simply this: keep it simple.

A good watch, some discreet diamond studs, and a carefully calibrated squirt of vintage perfume — the kind, with civet, that you almost can't find any more — and I was ready for action.

With a little luck, my date for the evening wouldn't show up in blue jeans and a tee-shirt.

I had agreed to meet Jack at MOMA, first to walk through the new sculpture exhibition and then to have a drink at the restaurant. Not only was he on time, but he was nicely turned out as well in a blue blazer, tan pants, and a decent white shirt. When he leaned forward to give me a kiss, I was pleased to discover that he smelled good, too.

Having already purchased our tickets, he confidently placed a proprietary arm on my shoulder and led us up two flights of stairs, where I quickly learned that he had done his homework.

During the next hour or so, I discovered that Jack didn't spend his entire intellectual life in the early nineteenth century. He talked knowledgeably and with animation about the history of sculpture, about the continuing tension between figuralism and abstraction, about the various processes that produced the objects we were looking at. And I also discovered that I wasn't just taking pleasure in studying him — I was enjoying being in his company as well.

When we walked down to the first floor again, I was nevertheless conscious of how Jack's clothing couldn't entirely disguise the fact that he was built more like a professional athlete than a promising art historian. You could see it in his neck and shoulders, in his barrel chest, in his muscular hands. He didn't have a heavy touch — far from it, in fact — but there was, I felt, an enormous amount of physical energy lying just below the surface. I could sense it in the directness of those speckled green eyes; I could see it as his decent white shirt rubbed lightly against his nipples. He was all there — and very, very focused.

Would a crisp glass of wine relax him a little? Not very much, as it turned out. Having provided a running commentary in the museum, he now began to ply me with questions. Where did I live in the city? Had I been married? What was my family like? How did they figure in the novels I had written?

I had to give him credit for unabashed directness. God knows I'm not used to it among the people with whom I normally hang out. And he had been reading my novels, although how thoroughly he could have digested them in less than a week's time was an open question — and one that he seemed to sidestep rather deftly.

'Our backgrounds are so different,' he commented, 'that it's amazing to me that we're both here sitting at the same bar together. I can't imagine what it must have been like to grow up in Boston. Are people there really as emotionally tight as the characters in your fiction?'

'Sometimes, Jack, they're even stiffer-upper-lip than I've described them to be — but if I portrayed them that way, no one would believe me.'

'And your own family?'

'My parents are wonderful, and I have lovely memories of most of my grandparents, all of them now departed. But push a little around the

99

edges —'

'Your siblings?' he asked.

'Not so much them as my uncles, aunts, and cousins. That's where the real stories lie.'

'Rather different in North Dakota,' he mused. 'There's certainly a lot of taciturnity — the Marlboro man kind of thing — but you know where you stand with people. They're direct, and they're sincere.

'And we have no "aunts" there,' he continued; 'only "ants."'

'Sorry about that. New Yorkers don't like our "aunts" very much either, although many of them certainly have their own way of mauling the language.'

'Having spent a couple of years in England, I suppose I should be used to these variations, but I'm afraid that "tomahtoes" still raises my hackles. Tell me, Abby, that you don't say "tomahtoes" yourself.'

'I'm going to have to plead guilty, I'm afraid,' I answered. 'I'm a very slowly recovering Yankee. But enough about me, as they used to say. Tell me what your experience at Oxford was like. Didn't someone tell me last weekend that you rowed for the university?'

'Not exactly,' he said. 'I rowed for my college and was in our first boat by the end of my second year, but I never rowed for Oxford itself. I was *supposed* to be a graduate student, remember?'

'And weren't you?'

'More or less. The nice thing about Oxford is the freedom you have and the sense of living somewhere completely different. It was like looking at the world through a new pair of glasses — and looking at America through those glasses as well.'

'And what did you see?' I asked.

'I'd say it was more a case of *how* I saw things. Less chauvinistically, in the first place. So much for "the American century." We still had a lot to learn about the rest of the world, and the students at Oxford will probably never forgive us for what we did in Vietnam — nor what we've more recently done in the Middle East.'

'But you weren't studying politics or economics there.'

'You know, Abby, before I arrived in England I thought that people in the humanities weren't really interested in politics or international relations, but after only a few months there I realized that everyone at Oxford had political and cultural opinions. *Strong* opinions, as I discovered. It was not always a comfortable situation, even for someone like me from the middle of nowhere.'

'Didn't people give you a pass on all of this? You personally — or even generationally — weren't responsible for anything.'

'Absolutely no passes, as I learned. You are

the representative – or scapegoat – at hand. If you are obtuse enough to wear a tie to dinner that has a fox head on it, as I once did, you will suffer the consequences. And I thought that I was being rather English by wearing the damn thing!'

'So you were — but perhaps a decade behind the times. We live and we learn, especially in a foreign culture, which I think England remains to this day. It isn't just that English is a common language that divides two nations, as someone once quipped. Desmond likes to argue that the old British class system, combined with the recent infusion of foreign capital and immigrants, has produced a topsy-turvy culture that simply doesn't know where its equilibrium lies any more. If, in fact, it still has any equilibrium left at all.'

'That's a nice way of putting it,' Jack said. 'I've more or less given up on analyzing my experience there, and although I've been able to return a few times to pursue my research in London, I've kept my distance from politics. Whenever I hear the words "New Labour" I want to vote for the neo-cons who have done their best to pollute our own country during the past decade or so.'

This was also nicely put, but there was anger in Jack's voice as well. Perhaps it was time, after two rounds of the crisp Alsatian, to face the music and dance.

'Jack,' I said, 'either you let me order us

some dinner or you're going to have to carry me home over your shoulder. What's it going to be?'

'Why not both?' he countered.

'Here?' I asked.

'It's your call.'

And so it was. I ordered up oysters on the half shell — certainly they couldn't take much time to prepare — and a medley of small lamb dishes to follow. The Alsatian would last us through the first course, and then some modest Merlot would finish us off. Depending, of course, on what we thought might follow.

I had made up my mind. I'd give this one a try. When the lamb was behind us and coffee was all that separated us from saying goodnight to each other, I leaned over to Jack at the bar and rubbed my lips against his ear.

'How far is your apartment from here?' he asked.

'Much too far,' I lied. 'And besides, I don't allow anyone to sleep with me there.'

'No one?'

'No one.'

'So what should we do?'

'How far is *your* place from here?' I asked.

'It's uptown, near Columbia, a long hike from here.'

'Is it presentable?' I asked.

'There's only one way to find out.'

'On one condition,' I added.

'And what's that?'

'I call the shots — completely.'

He took a few moments to think about this, and then rubbed his lips against my ear and quietly murmured, 'okay.'

But that didn't mean, of course, that he would completely behave himself in the cab as we slowly jolted northward. I tried to cool him down with some playful kissing, hoping that our driver would turn a blind eye – if, in fact, you want your cabby to have a blind eye to turn.

Two surprises lay ahead. The first was that Jack's studio apartment, small as it was, enjoyed a remarkably nice view of the Hudson River and the surrounding neighborhood. The second — and I suppose this shouldn't have been a surprise at all by this point — was that he clearly had a sense of design. If anything, one might say that his place was almost too well ordered, too tidy and tucked-in.

'I hope it's presentable,' he said with a somewhat nervous smile. 'There's certainly not much here to present.'

'You have the essentials, and that's all that counts: your books, a bed, and a view. What more could a girl want?'

'Something to drink, I imagine,' he said.

'Something light. What do you have?'

'I have some white wine, or I can make us gin and tonics.'

'After what I went through in the cab,' I said, 'I think I deserve a gin and tonic.'

While he went to work in the small galley kitchen, I surveyed his apartment once again. The bed was made — thank God! — and the few pieces of furniture had obviously been chosen with care: a sofa, a club chair, and a small table that doubled as a desk. All very modern, and clean as a whistle.

Most of the room, however, was given over to books — probably a thousand or so in all — arranged by size and subject and housed in a minimalist structure that seemed to be wired to the walls. Sculpture, landscape, portraiture, printmaking, drawings, photography, film, the entire gamut of English literature, modern fiction, critical theory: it was all pretty much there, the foundation of an art historian's working library. And it included, I noticed, not only my two slim volumes (in hardcover, no less), but a copy of Desi's book on Baroque portraiture as well.

Jack made two quite respectable drinks, and as I began to sip mine, he asked me when I was going to take charge. 'Right now,' I answered.

'And what if I don't submit?'

'Then I'll pick up my marbles and go home.'

'And what if it hurts?'

'It won't. It's pure pleasure — nothing more, and nothing less.'

I was, of course, true to my word. I removed

my dress and thong (only my heels and lipstick remained). I slowly stripped him (there was much to admire). I took my time teasing him (he needed little of that). I pinned him to the bed (much to his surprise) and then gave us both a long, hard ride. And then, at his request, another. Oh to be twenty-something again!

Before I left — and as Jack was recovering from what he referred to as his 'ordeal' — he offered to take me someplace in the neighborhood for dessert. I was a tad hungry again by this point, but I politely declined. Enough was just right. When I arrived home, I took a long hot shower, put on my bathrobe, and began to make myself some tea. It was only then that I saw that the light on my phone machine was steadily blinking at me. I hesitated, but then decided to listen to the message.

It was Desi.

'Sorry, Abby; something's come up and we should talk whenever you receive this. I'm at home.' I didn't like the sound of his voice, which made me feel a little panicky in the pit of my stomach.

I took a deep breath and then gave him a call.

'Abby, I have some very bad news, I'm afraid. Can I come 'round and pick you up?'

'That's okay, Desi. I'll take a cab and be there in a few minutes. But what's the matter? You can tell me now.'

'It's David. He's been found dead, Abby.'
'Found dead? David?'
'Yes, Abby. He's been murdered.'

Friday – Sunday, 21-23 September

Although I had not known David very long, not nearly as long as Desi had, I felt a powerful combination of grief and injustice – and of fear, for violent forces had somehow penetrated the breaches of our seemingly safe and tranquil world.

Desi knew very little about the circumstances of David's death when I arrived at the carriage house. The news had hit him hard, and we spent most of an hour simply holding each other and asking ourselves how anyone could possibly have wanted to hurt someone as kind as David.

We both took a light sleeping pill and then faced the world again over coffee the next morning, a Friday. Desi had received a call late in the afternoon on Thursday from David's friend Richard Yung. David, Desi learned, had not shown up for work at the Met on Wednesday. No one thought much of it except for Richard, who was supposed to meet him for lunch and hadn't received a call from David to say that he wasn't able to keep their engagement. David didn't answer the phone at home, nor did he show up for work on Thursday morning, so Richard contacted the Met's security force, which in turn was in touch with the local police station in Greenwich Village. The door to David's apartment was locked, but the super let the police in — and together they discovered his body. This was all that Richard knew.

'What,' I asked Desi over breakfast, 'can *we* do?'

'I'll call my friend Stephen at the Met and be of whatever assistance I can. It's possible that he can shed some light. Was there anything going on with David? He might know. And I could offer to call David's parents in Minneapolis, though no doubt the police have already done so. I've met them only once, but I can begin to imagine how devastated they must be. I'll do whatever I can to help them, of course, but it's going to be a very difficult time for them.'

'And what about me?'

'Try to stay busy, Abby. It's hard, I know, but sometimes focusing on work really helps you get through something like this.'

'Do you still want to think about going out to the Island tomorrow?'

'Let's see what there is to learn here first. We could always make a late weekend of it if we wanted to.'

I spent most of the day talking unproductively with friends, returning my mother's call from two days ago, and arranging lunch with Patricia Simmons for the following week. When Jack Springer called to say hello, he instantly pulled back from suggesting an immediate rendezvous, for which I was grateful. My God, I thought to myself: I had met him at MOMA less than twenty-four hours ago. How quickly a girl's emotional landscape can change.

I met Renata for a quick coffee to relay the news. She was horrified. 'I only met him last weekend, but you could tell immediately that he was such a lovely guy. Who would want to harm someone as nice as David?'

That, of course, was the million-dollar question. It made no sense at all. He was studious, unassuming – hard to imagine any explanation other than a speculative burglary gone wrong.

I had agreed to shop for dinner and I kept it simple: some Porterhouses on the grill on Desi's terrace, roasted beets, some late Vidalia onions that were still in season — and then a salad and some fresh fruit. When he arrived home I gave him a soft kiss, mixed some very welcome martinis for both of us, and waited anxiously to hear what he had learned. It was less than I had expected.

'It's something of a catch-22 situation,' he told me. 'It was good to talk to Stephen – who can't tell us anything new, by the way – but trying to talk to the police is much more difficult. The detective in charge of the investigation has been in touch, but at this point I suppose I'm as much a suspect as anyone else, even though it's not yet clear if they know whether or not David was murdered. And I can't blame them for being suspicious — nor for moving with extreme caution.'

'I should think so. How familiar can they be with the world of gay art historians?'

'Indeed. But he wasn't unusual in that sense. He lived in the Village, had a close circle of friends, a job in the arts. He didn't really stand out. In any case, I'm hoping to hear more from our detective sergeant tomorrow.'

'So we should stay put this weekend?' I asked.

'I think so, Abby. Let's see what transpires tomorrow.'

And so we settled into a leisurely dinner and an old screwball comedy from the late 1930s, and then an early bedtime.

Saturday brought, at last, some information about David's last hours. Desi had been interviewed at length by the police and looked drained. I made rum and tonics while he took a quick shower and changed, and then we walked a few blocks to a small bistro we like for a quiet, simple supper.

'The officer in charge is an impressive type,'

Desi began once we'd sat down and ordered two glasses of a crisp Sancerre. 'Sergeant Mullins has been around the block a few times — and then some. He didn't give a lot away, but I think it helped that several people at the museum had mentioned my name as someone to talk to. In any case, it appears that someone was seen going into David's apartment Tuesday evening and that David was dead shortly afterwards.'

'So it wasn't a break-in?' I asked.

'No, apparently not. No sign of forced entry. There had been a struggle, however, and the apartment was torn up a bit.'

'Was anything stolen? Did David own anything valuable?'

'Well, I think they're finding it hard to figure that out. Very few people had been to David's apartment, so it's difficult to determine just what he owned without going through all of his records first.'

'Surely Richard had been there?'

'You would think so, wouldn't you? But Mullins wasn't very forthcoming about the details. But what he did say seems to tally with what Richard told me on the phone the other night. I should go and see him tomorrow. He must be in a terrible state. Do you want to join me?'

'Of course. Perhaps we should invite him for brunch tomorrow. Do you have his number?'

Desi did, so I gave him my phone and he left a

brief message for Richard.

'What next?' I asked.

'With all this going on, I've rather lost my appetite the last couple of days. What looks good to you?' he said as he flicked out his napkin to the side of him like a toreador, before smoothing it onto his lap. 'I think I may order the fish soup and then something light, perhaps a *salade Niçoise* with plenty of fresh white anchovies.'

'Sounds virtuous. I'll just have a taste of your soup and then dig into a *daube*. The dish always sounds so autumnal.'

'We had beef last night, remember?'

'Yes, but this is beef cheek, Dr. Fairbrother. Altogether different.'

'*Touché*, my dear. I'll even let you order the red wine this evening.'

We went to bed early once again. Both of us were feeling rather *sotto voce*, and I knew that Desi was also frustrated by not being able to further the investigation by much. But instead of immediately falling asleep, we spent some time in the dark talking to each other, and then giving each other a long, slow massage. More erotic activities could wait until the morning.

And so they did. When we had pleasured each other and drunk enough coffee to start the day, we stepped into Desi's wonderful walk-in shower and gave each other a thorough scrubbing. Just as we finished our ritual, the phone rang and Desi confirmed an appointment for brunch with Richard Yung. If it was warm enough, we would sit outside on the terrace and enjoy the autumnal sun.

Richard arrived around eleven, looking as if he was in need of sleep but otherwise in better spirits than I had expected. Desi poured us some fresh iced tea and we sat together outside, off the back of the kitchen, taking advantage of the nice weather while it lasted. I had made a quick run to the local food emporium and procured us a selection of antipasti and some fresh vegetables and eggs, which Desi would scramble according to a much-loved recipe in his much-thumbed copy of the Nero Wolfe cookbook: as slowly as one can, in a double boiler, with just the right fresh herbs.

But our focus was clearly on Richard, and he was eager to have friends with whom to talk.

'It's a fairly weird situation,' he began. 'I mean, I really want to help the police, you know, to piece together what's happened – but at the same time, I was his lover and one of the very few visitors to his apartment. So how does that look! They seem very interested in his collection – and I don't know the first thing about it, of course – but I suppose they don't have any other motive.'

'Was there anything going on with David? Had you noticed anything different?' I asked.

'Yes and no. He is,' Richard began, and then

caught himself: 'sorry, I should say he was a pretty even-tempered person. But he was a bit irritable on Sunday as we made our way back to the city, and continued to be so when I saw him at the museum early in the week. Not mean-spirited or anything like that, but clearly exercised about something.'

'Do you know why?' Desi asked.

'I'm not entirely sure. But he seemed to be a bit jealous of Andrew Cameron, you know, who we met for the first time in Sag Harbor at your weekend dinner. Andy and I hit it off pretty well — much more so than Andy did with David — and David made a few remarks to me about Andy that weren't very flattering.'

'When was this?' Desi continued.

'On Sunday, as we came back to New York.'

'And what about during the week?' I asked.

'On Tuesday, when I stopped by his office, he asked me whether I was going to see Andy at some point.'

Richard looked at us both carefully and saw the next question written on our faces.

'And so I told him that I didn't have any plans to do so, but that I felt I had the right to see him if I wished to.'

'Did you?' Desi asked.

'No. Not yet. But that may change.'

'Have you told him about what happened?' I asked.

'I didn't do so immediately. But when it was clear that the news was going to come out in the papers, I gave him a call.'

'And his reaction?' I pressed on.

'He was stunned. Really shocked, like everybody else. He offered to come see me, but I told him that it would be better to wait.'

'Have the police talked with him?' I asked.

'I don't know. But I did tell the sergeant about Andy, so he may do so at some point.'

'Was it typical of David,' Desi asked, 'to be jealous of someone else?'

'I don't know,' Richard answered. 'We hadn't been seeing each other for more than a couple of months, and it hadn't ever come up. He certainly knew that I had had several boyfriends, and I never thought of him as being prudish. It was just the way things are, and he seemed to accept it.' Desi got up and went to the kitchen.

'I hope we're not prying too much,' Desi continued as he came back with some refreshed glasses and the platter of antipasti. 'We're just trying to make sense of these things ourselves. But had you seen other people during the two months you were with David? And, by the way, I'm not being remotely judgmental, believe me.' Desi blinked at me, giving nothing away.

'Yes and no. I wasn't carrying on a second relationship, if that's what you mean. But I'm still friends with some of my former lovers, and I saw a couple of them during this period. Nothing serious: just a drink or a dinner or a movie. Nothing that would have gotten in the way of my relationship with David.'

'Did the police give you any sense of when, exactly, David was killed?' I asked, taking a sip of iced tea.

'All I know is that it was sometime on Tuesday evening, based on the questions he was asking me.'

'And do you have a firm alibi?' Desi asked.

'Not really. I was working at home on a curatorial project. But I did make a few phone calls, including one to David, which he didn't answer.'

And so our conversation continued as we finished our antipasti and retreated to the kitchen so that Desi could slow-scramble his eggs. Neither of us wanted to play the rough-and-tumble cross-examiner, especially with someone who clearly cared for David and was a bit worn down by the police interrogation he had gone through and the uncertainty that followed it. And there seemed to be little more to be learned. Before he left, however, Richard thanked Desi for what he had written in the brief obit that had appeared in the *Times*. 'It was the least I could do,' Desi responded. 'He was a very promising young scholar and it gave me real pleasure to pay tribute to him. His parents, I hope, will take some consolation in discovering just how much he was admired as well as liked.'

After Richard had left, I remarked on how gentle Desi had been, treating him with kid gloves.

'He's a nice young man,' he replied, 'and I doubt whether his story is fundamentally flawed. But much as I wanted to press him on several points, that actually remains, I think, the proper domain of the police. Perhaps we can find out when, precisely, Richard last saw David, or when, exactly, he called him on Tuesday evening. Richard said that he had told David that he had no plans to see Andy. That's not exactly the same as saying that he had *not* yet seen him — or, for that matter, had seen him sometime after their conversation on the Sunday. In the meantime, we've cheered him up a bit and let him know that we're sympathetic. If the police have no other real suspects, he's clearly in an awkward situation.'

'Come on, let's do something. Is it too late to cycle to the ferry and make our usual loop around Staten Island?' I asked.

'We may not be able to make the circuit, but at the very worst we can break the bikes down and put them in a large cab on the way back. That's why the gods of Gotham invented taxicabs, after all.'

'How could I forget?'

Many of Desi's friends — and even more so

his distant admirers, I imagine — must think that their learned friend and generous host does nothing but stare closely at sumptuous objects and peruse erudite books. Even those who know something about his sexual conquests probably imagine that his athletic activity is confined to the more erotic forms of physical exertion. I don't want to take anything away from those exertions, having enjoyed a large measure of them myself, but the simple fact is that Desmond Fairbrother is — yes, I must confess it — a closet athlete.

Very closeted. He didn't row at Oxford or play competitive squash in graduate school, mind you, but he does work hard to keep himself in good shape. But not in a local gym or fitness center, I assure you. Desi has a small space tucked off the upstairs bathroom, equipped with a treadmill, a spinning machine, and various forms of muscular torture. Just as importantly, he has invested in a superb high fidelity system and video ensemble that would give a Hollywood magnate's private screening room a decent run for the money. It's an indulgence, of course, but it's the only television in the house, and it enables Desi to watch documentaries or listen to opera whenever he has a chance to punctuate his day.

But not on this Sunday, which was devoted to fresh air and the cyclist's discipline of concentrating carefully on automobiles, flashing lights, and the other hazards of the road. The traffic was fairly light, and the ferry over to Staten Island enabled us to relax as we enjoyed the sheer visual pageantry of the harbor and its late-September voyagers: sailboats, pleasure boats, tugs, and other ferries, with the inevitable planes and helicopters overhead. It always reminds me of those children's books that made the metropolis look like a crazy maze of roads and railroad tracks and bridges with primitive airplanes flying perilously underneath them.

Staten Island proved to offer just the respite we needed and just the right amount of exercise. It was such an emotional release to be able to focus on nothing but our bodies and our breathing as we worked the gears and gauged how to maximize our energy.

The light held until we reached the ferry again, and we prudently hailed a large cab when we were safely back on *terra manhattaniensis*. When we had wheeled our bicycles into the storage room and stripped ourselves of our colorful cycling gear in the kitchen, Desi gave me a long kiss and then licked the salt off of several prominent parts of my still sweating body.

'I needed that,' he whispered.

'You've left the best for last,' I responded, and then asked him what he wanted to drink.

We took a pitcher of ice water and a shaker of vodka martinis up to the bathroom and drew some hot water in the chaste white tub he had mounted in the center of the room. Nothing orgiastic: just enough room for two healthy adults — and whatever provisions one might need.

As we slipped into the billowing suds and began to drink our water, Desi gave me both a sweet smile and a meaningful look at the same time. 'You know, Abby,' he said, 'we're doing our very best to carry on business as usual — perhaps I should say life as usual — but nothing really seems usual anymore. David's death may be behind us, but not the mystery surrounding it.

'I may be getting in way over my head, but I think I have an obligation to myself to do whatever I can to solve it. It's not that I mistrust the work of the police; it's just that I sense that there's something complicated going on here, possibly related to David's collecting, the kind of thing that the police may not twig to. And I think I'll feel incredibly frustrated if I don't take some positive steps to sort things out.'

'On your own?' I asked, with a frown I couldn't quite conceal.

'Working with the police, of course, but perhaps on my own hook as well.'

'What do you have in mind, Desi?' I continued, as I poured us each a glass of our ice-cold concoction from the crystal shaker.

'Well, in the first place I want to construct an outline of what happened and when. There's not much information at this point, but perhaps

Sergeant Mullins will be able to fill me in a bit more fully tomorrow.

'And then, in the second place, it may be useful to divide the possible suspects into three groups.'

'*Perché tre?*'

'Simple triangulation. You and I are quite capable of talking to and thinking about the three youngsters with whom David partied this past weekend. They're among the people he saw immediately before he died, and we therefore have to consider them very carefully. The police, of course, are naturally intrigued by Richard, but they might be equally intrigued by Andy, if in fact he was quickly sucked into the dynamics of Richard's relationship with David.'

'Which Richard denies.'

'So he does. And with a little luck the police may be able to support his statements.'

'What about Jack Springer?' I asked.

'Well,' Desi replied, 'he doesn't seem to share David's sexual predilections, does he?'

'Is that a rhetorical question, Dr. Fairbrother?'

'Is that a rhetorical answer, Miss Higginson?'

'Fair enough, darling. He is, in my opinion and limited experience, decidedly in the hetero camp.'

'I certainly can't hold that against him, although his taste in propositioning proper New England hostesses at the kitchen sink might strike a chap as being more than a bit uncouth.'

'Fair enough. Pray continue.'

'And then there's the second group, which consists of fellow curators and other museum colleagues who knew David, both those at the Met — many of whom must have seen him at the beginning of the week — and those who work elsewhere. This is one area where I might be able to work with the police as they extend their dragnet and begin to talk to people.'

'And the third group?'

'Well, that's the largest and most mysterious of all. And I suppose it's the group that only a proper police investigation can handle.'

'You mean the people we know nothing about?' I asked.

'Precisely. Other friends. Former lovers — if David had any here. And then the entire bar scene in the Village, which may have led to an encounter back in David's apartment.'

'That sounds like searching for the proverbial needle,' I said.

'Well, I imagine that this particular haystack has been searched many times before. In any case, I hope to find out more tomorrow.'

'And what about tonight?'

We were stretched out across from each other in the bathtub, and I had one foot lightly placed on Desi's stomach and the other strategically placed beneath his landing gear.

'If I remember correctly,' he replied, 'we have unfinished business of a Latinate nature. Would you like to take your pleasure right here and now?'

'Now — but not here,' I said. 'I want you to turn on the heat in your sauna, *s'il te plaît.*'

By the time we were finished, my legs were almost too wobbly to stand on. 'Take a bit of this, old girl,' he whispered, offering me the remainder of my much-needed martini.

'Only one thing would have made it better,' he added.

'And what's *that*?' I demanded.

'Some of your stilettos, of course.'

'They don't make them in plastic,' I answered. 'Or do they?'

'Of course they do. I'll find you some tomorrow.'

'In black, please. And if you're really good,' I sighed, 'I'll even let you paint my toenails red.'

Monday – Tuesday, 24-25 September

So much for the sabbath! We now had a very busy week ahead of us. Desi was scheduled to meet with Mullins on Monday, just as I headed off to my apartment for the first time in several days. As I left, he asked me for Renata's telephone number at work. I arched an eyebrow as dramatically as I could, but I said nothing as I wrote it out for him on one of the cards in my red-and-black jotter. On Tuesday Desi would spend most of the afternoon talking to interior designers in New York, followed by a cocktail party for them at his carriage house. I had agreed to stay for the festivities, but that prompted me to ask Desi if I might sit in on his session with the decorators, even if I were a bit late.

I might well be late, mind you, because I had scheduled my lunch with Patricia Simmons for Tuesday as well. I still wasn't sure, on the other hand, what to do about Jack. He was polite but insistent, leaving me two more phone messages over the weekend. I gave him a call when I returned to my apartment and offered to have a drink with him later in the week. I tried to keep it fairly low key, but nothing about Jack seemed to be fairly low key.

In the meantime I had begun to block out the themes I wanted to approach in my lunch with Patricia. Why would people wish to live there, in a relatively undeveloped part of the city? How did they decide to introduce contemporary art into such a demonstrably traditional setting? Why would anyone wish to sell art out of their own apartment? What impassioned them about art in the first place? How do they choose the objects they intend to sell? What do they collect for themselves — and keep? What is the relationship between dealing in art and working in the financial sector? And why is there a very beautiful late-eighteenth-century painting hanging in milady's boudoir? Enough questions, I thought, to get the creative juices flowing, at least for now.

I had suggested that she meet me at a chic Italian restaurant fairly north on Madison. The food is very good there and the pastries and espresso are perhaps the best in the city. Patricia arrived spot-on at one and we spent a few minutes taking each other in as we ordered a glass of wine and made ourselves comfortable. She was just as attractive and stylish as I had remembered, dressed in a black cashmere turtleneck sweater, sleek gray trousers, Italian flats, and a simple medley of pearls: earrings, two strands around her neck, and a lovely bracelet that she wore on the outside of her sweater. She presented a striking rather than a precisely beautiful face, with prominent cheekbones and sharp, sensuous lips that eschewed the makeup they clearly didn't need.

Et moi? I had decided to wear black pants, an embroidered white blouse Desi's shirtmaker had made for me, a coral necklace, a vintage watch with a red leather strap, and red heels. We carefully looked each other over and – I would say – silently approved of each other's choice.

Patricia, as it turned out, was more than willing to be drawn out about the design and collecting choices she had made with her husband. She seemed to treat their newest venture as something short of an actual business proposition; she thought of it more as a playful experiment that had suddenly taken wing.

'Ronald,' she explained, 'is one of those people who always needs to have something new on the horizon. He wakes up each morning or comes home each evening with several new ideas, all of them interesting, some of them so counter-intuitive that you wonder where on earth his mind has been wandering while the rest of us have been pursuing our normal routines.'

'Is that something you find stimulating,' I asked, 'or does it drive you crazy?'

'Well, you either resist it, which leads directly to the domestic relations lawyer, or you stand back until the coast is clear and then try to channel some of that energy in a productive way. That's essentially how we began this new project. Ronald wanted to do something on the side that wasn't purely financial; he wanted something tangible — material — to be part of the mix. My job was to define what the "stuff" ought to be.'

'Was that difficult?' I asked.

'Well, I was easily drawn to art; we already collected contemporary paintings and sculpture and we enjoy placing them in our apartment as well as in our place in the country. The difficult part was convincing Ronald that we should buy in order to sell. But once he was willing to entertain the idea, he quickly came up with the suggestion that we place the art works in a setting that was quite unlike all of the postmodern galleries everyone goes to.'

'Are you pleased so far?' I looked her directly in the eye to gauge the reaction.

'Absolutely. The media coverage has been great and we've sold quite a few pieces in the first month or so.'

'Sorry,' I quickly interrupted. 'I meant to ask whether you've been pleased by the concept — selling out of your own home, and juxtaposing the edgy artwork against your traditional architecture.'

She paused a moment and then gave me a somewhat quizzical look. 'Well, Abby, I suppose it depends on how you define the word "home."'

'Home is where your heart is,' I responded. 'Home is where the bills arrive. Home is where you live, at least part of the time.'

'Then, strictly speaking,' she said, 'home remains our apartment on the Upper West Side.'

I needed a moment to take this in.

'You mean,' I asked, 'you haven't sold your other place and moved into the apartment in Chelsea?'

'Yes and no. We've restored the new apartment, we've completely furnished it, we've moved some of our clothing there, and we enjoy entertaining there.'

'But . . .' I added.

'But we've kept our old apartment — which, by the way, is more modern than the one in Chelsea. And we still have our place in Westchester, also quite modern.'

'And the heart and the bills, where do they belong?' I asked.

'On the Upper West Side.'

'So,' I continued, 'your new apartment is more or less a theatrical contrivance? A stage set for art and commerce?'

'You could put it that way, I suppose. Ronald thinks of it as an investment. I suppose that I think of it as a third home. Or perhaps, strictly speaking, a fourth.'

'A fourth?' I asked.

'Can we talk off the record for a moment?' She twirled a rather handsome earring, tilting her head to one side.

'Of course.'

'Good. You see, when Ronald asked me to marry him, I did so with a number of stipulations that were important to me — and they still are. No children. Financial independence. A certain amount of social independence. And a flat in Paris. No questions asked.'

'And your power-broker accepted all of your articles of convention?'

'And signed on the dotted line. Believe me, it's made life much easier for both of us. And besides, he's got a daughter from his first marriage, lots of business friends, and — as you can see — enough energy for all of us.'

'Why Paris?' I asked.

'Why not!' she answered. 'Seriously, though, it was a form of compensation I paid myself for giving up my graduate studies at the Institute.'

'Was that a tough decision to make?'

'Not at the time; only later did I realize what I was missing. And by that time it was too late. I was too successful to return to it.'

'Successful at what?' I asked, intrigued and yet put off by the arrogance behind her remark.

Another moment of silence.

'Didn't you know that I was a model?' she finally answered.

'Are we on the record again?' I asked.

'Of course.'

'Then the answer, in all honesty, is no. I thought that you were a graduate student in art history.'

'I was. But that wasn't the person Ronald Simmons fell for. You see, I came to the Institute on a scholarship, but living in New York turned out to be very expensive and I didn't want to commute to the Bronx or Hackensack like my compatriots. Someone suggested that I should take part in a modeling competition that was featured in an arts benefit of some kind, and a few days later I had a part-time job with a local agency. Mostly it was work for the seasonal clothing catalogs, but sometimes it actually involved walking down a runway. In any case, one thing led to another, and I was eventually noticed by someone at a larger agency who offered me a full-time exclusive contract. The rest is history — or at least my history.'

'I had no idea,' I said. 'So how long did you grace the runways?'

'Almost seven years. You don't have a very long shelf-life in the modeling business, so I had a pretty good run. I met a lot of interesting people . . .'

'Including other models?' I couldn't help but

ask.

'Yes, many of them were quite interesting. Not intellectually, mind you, but some of them were very intelligent and many of them had a great sense of style. And then, of course, there were the extreme narcissists and those who had absolutely no self-confidence whatsoever — but you could avoid them easily enough.'

'You must have had your admirers,' I continued.

'A few, yes, but you have to think carefully about what men want when they ask you out. They know virtually nothing about you as a person, and I suppose that for some men that's perfectly all right. They're excited by the glamour and reified sexuality of it all.'

'Reified sexuality,' I repeated. 'I'd like to use that.'

'Be my guest. But — to continue my miniseries — I can't tell you how many men were turned off when they discovered that I had been a graduate student and actually cared a good deal about my subject. The "what-I-see-is-what-I-get" syndrome runs very deep, I soon realized.

'And that,' she added, 'is why Desmond Fairbrother was drooled over so fervently at the Institute. You knew that you were being intellectually challenged, that you were being trained to see things in different ways. But the fact that he was gorgeous on top of it all was really too much for most of the female graduate students. They wanted him lock, stock, and barrel.'

'The diffident star of the art historical runway?' I asked while feeling uncomfortably proprietorial.

'Very much so, and yet the women were shockingly forward. And his lack of "availability" to his students was, I suppose, a powerful inducement for many of them to get their degrees!'

'Well put,' I replied, smirking inwardly, and quietly proud that I had stormed that particular citadel.

'That, and his little intrigues,' she added with a sly smile.

'What do mean, "his little intrigues"?' I shifted in my seat and took a sip of wine.

'Oh, come on. You must know about the little mystery Desmond solved at the Institute? Though, it's true, he was never very forthcoming about it.'

'You'll have to enlighten me.' I wasn't enjoying the sensation that she knew more about Desi than I did.

'As I remember it, one of the young assistant professors was being harassed in a series of anonymous letters in his mailbox. Everyone, including the director, seemed to think that one of the other assistant professors – one of his rivals – was responsible. But Desmond convinced the director that he was wrong by proving that the letters had actually been written by a senior member of the faculty. And the reason Desmond may not wish to talk about it is because this senior colleague had taken your friend under his wing, so to speak, so it was a delicate situation which Desmond handled with considerable diplomacy.'

'Sounds like Desmond. He can't abide injustice. I take it that you weren't among the slavishly devout?'

'No, that's not my style. I worked hard, and yet I'm not sure whether Desmond even noticed me.'

'He did, in fact,' I answered, unwilling to give anything more away.

'Well, better late than never! So, Abby, how long have you and Desmond been together?'

'"Together" is probably not the operative word. Let's say that we've been an item off and on for over fifteen years.'

'Off and on?' she asked.

'Well, we haven't always lived in the same city — or country — and we've never lived together.'

'But you've been "together" some time, no?' She indicated the quotation marks with her index fingers.

'For almost a decade. We met as I was finishing my undergraduate work in Cambridge, but I then spent two years studying in Paris. I then returned to Boston for several years and worked in a publishing house before New York — and Desmond — extended their welcoming arms to an errant Yankee yearning to breathe free.'

'And so you now have all the prizes, male as well as literary?' she quipped.

'Not exactly, Patricia,' I pushed back. 'I've made a short-list or two, but so far the prize itself has eluded me. And as for Dr. Fairbrother,' I added, 'he lives his own life as well as ours.'

'So I understand,' she said. 'It sounds as if Ronald and I are not the only ones to have such civilized understandings. And therefore,' she continued, 'I suppose that it's possible for someone like me still to have a shot at the prize?'

I hope that my jaw didn't noticeably drop, nor that I missed many beats before making as diplomatic an answer as I could. 'You have excellent taste in virtually everything, Patricia; I'm sure that Desmond would find you to be a worthy challenge.'

'The challenge I have in mind, Abby, is a little more complicated than that,' she responded.

Where, I wondered, was she possibly headed? And whose interview was this, anyway?

'What I find particularly exciting is the combination the two of you make: socially, stylishly, sexually.'

She drew out these final three words to great

dramatic effect: 'socially, stylishly, sexually.' It was my turn to smile — and be speechless.

'Think it over,' she whispered as she rose from her seat and headed for the ladies' room.

I paid the bill and then joined her as we walked through the restaurant to the street. As we parted, she turned to give me what I thought would be the inevitable air kiss on both cheeks.

Instead, she brushed her lips against mine and softly murmured 'think it over' once again.

Tuesday, 25 September

It was now a bit after three o'clock and I was sure that the program was well underway. When I arrived at the swank hotel further south on the East Side, however, I was told that the speaker was just being introduced. And was I Abigail Higginson, I was asked? An envelope awaited me, inside of which was a note from our friend Robert Linardo, informing me that he had saved a seat near the rear of the ballroom next to his. Thoughtfulness personified, as always.

I easily found Robert and gave him an appreciative kiss.

'Lovely entrance,' he whispered. 'And you're not even that late. Remember, my dear, we're on decorators' time here!'

I always enjoy seeing how people struggle to introduce Desi on such occasions. This afternoon, however, I had missed the introduction altogether, but it didn't make any difference, I soon discovered, because Desi was going to begin his presentation by addressing the subject head-on, as he likes to do.

I think that I know Desi's spiel almost by heart. He usually begins by complimenting these pampered interior decorators for turning 'houses into homes,' as his mother used to say, and then placing his own work somewhere between what *they* do and what he *used* to do at the Institute – teaching, and writing essays and books on art history. His main job now is to help individuals and institutions build collections of art, sometimes on a very small scale, sometimes not!

'I'm not a dealer,' I now heard him remind them. 'Nor am I an agent for dealers. And I'm certainly not a designer. That's your job, and I enjoy working with my friends in the design world when they wish to have my particular kind of advice. Some of these friends think of me as a facilitator, and it's true that I sometimes broker transactions that involve owners, dealers, designers, and their clients. But I can only facilitate in areas where I have a certain amount of knowledge, and that's why my friends sometimes have recourse to the rather old-fashioned moniker of "connoisseur" when they describe what I do. And after resisting it for some time, I now think that it's as useful a descriptor as anything else I've been fettered with. A few of which,' he remarked, 'are not necessarily very complimentary.'

Desi was now off and running, gracefully

stroking the professional egos of perhaps two hundred men and women who were dressed to the nines and who — as he carefully proceeded — seemed increasingly willing to entertain his central proposition. The moment a client engages the services of a designer, he argued, is also the moment when a client's art collection should be seriously appraised. Designers already do this when they assess their client's furniture — and they also think carefully about the relationship of existing works of art to whatever new or renovated space is being created. What Desi urged them to consider was the relative strength or weakness of these works of art as a collection unto itself. Does it have integrity? Can it be augmented or edited? In addition to thinking about new works of art that would provide the right visual elements in a room, Desi encouraged his audience to think about the purchase of additional paintings, prints, or statues that would solidify the collection per se. 'As a profession,' he told them, 'you have transformed yourselves from decorators into designers. And I now want you to consider transforming yourselves from designers into curators — or at least to shoulder both roles at the same time.

'May I have the lights dimmed, please.'

What followed, much to the audience's delight, was a series of case studies in which Desi produced before-and-after photographs of four different projects and carefully documented the process by which he had worked with individual designers and their clients. He didn't name names, of course, but some of the designers' work was easily identifiable, including that of dear Robert, who purred throughout this part of the performance.

It was an ambitious presentation, but Desi held his audience's attention for almost an hour and then answered a torrent of questions with his lightest touch. How do you structure your fees? How do you deal with clients who don't collect — or who don't think of themselves as collectors? How do you convince clients to sell or give away works that have sentimental value for them? What do you think of mixing the old and the new? And so on — and so on.

Robert and I left as soon as the final applause was over, knowing that Desi would be overtaken by friends in the audience and that someone should be ready to greet his guests when they made their way to the carriage house.

'Perfect, just perfect!' Robert cried when we were safely in a cab. 'Desmond had them in the palm of his hand, don't you think?'

'He was certainly in his element, Robert. And he seemed to be enjoying himself as well. Once a teacher, always a teacher, right?'

'And the best part, Abby,' he continued, 'is that the final photographs for each project not only revealed stronger collections in each case, but they also showed off better rooms as well. And that's the message each designer will take away from the program today.'

'And now, dear Robert,' I added, 'they have the opportunity to see just what Desmond's done for himself as well.'

I've hosted dozens of parties with Desi over the years, but I don't think that I've ever presided over a larger or noisier one — as if anyone could preside over anything in such a crowd!

'This is the best-dressed contingent we've ever seen here, Robert,' I told him half an hour later, trying not to shout.

'And the largest concentration of fragrance per square inch in all of Manhattan,' he volleyed back.

It appeared as if virtually everyone in Desi's audience had found their way to his door, and we had invited a few of our own friends as well. Renata had brought Jeremy, John Hawes had brought the scintillating Dolores (in red this evening), and Dennis and Madeleine stopped by as well. I spied several other familiar faces from afar, but the crowd was so large that Desi had opened the terrace in back and the library upstairs to take care of the overflow. Waiters were stationed everywhere — and they were needed, for security as well as for the constant flow of drinks. Most of our own friends left well before the reveling designers, who finally deserted the ramparts around nine.

'My God, Desi,' I exclaimed as the last guests danced through the door, 'is that really you?'

'I'm sorry, my dear,' he said. 'Have I even blown you a kiss this evening? This may be one party we needn't repeat anytime soon.'

'How, Dr. Fairbrother, could an event as civilized as your presentation lead to such a bacchanal? Who *are* these people?'

'They're very creative individuals who also know how to party as if there's no tomorrow. And if you think that this is the end of the party for them, I assure you that they've got further plans up their designer sleeves.

'I do, however,' he added, 'have at least one small surprise for you.' As the waiters continued to collect the glassware and tidy the rooms, Desi led me into the kitchen, where two place settings had been laid out on the granite island in the center of the room. Flowers from the living room had been placed in the middle of the island, and a bottle of Pétrus had been decanted into one of the antique carafes.

'This is lovely, Desi,' I cooed. 'And I deserve every bit of it!'

A waiter came by and handed us glasses of champagne in large flutes.

'Well, I thought that as long as we had the waiters and the caterer, we might as well keep them for an additional hour or so. Jules is cooking us some sea bass encased in rock salt, with wilted greens, slow-cooked tomatoes, and caramelized onions. And three kinds of *sorbetti* for dessert. I hope you enjoy my little *sorpresa*; you've been a trooper today, and I appreciate it.'

'Oh, darling,' I responded, 'you have no idea what a trooper I've been. I deserve a frigging congressional commendation.'

'Use your grown-up words, my dear.'

'But let's wait until the morning to share our various secrets. I rather like being surrounded by fifteen young men in black tie and our wonderful Jules wearing his heavenly toque.

'And the Pétrus!' I added. 'You're absolutely spoiling me.'

'Of course I am,' Desi said with his mischievous smile. 'But if history is an accurate predictor of future behavior, you'll soon get over it.'

Wednesday – Thursday,
26-27 September

I would have loved to sleep in on Wednesday
morning, but there was no extended rest for the
wicked or the merely weary. Desi made coffee
and we then worked out in his fitness room,
watching the first act of a newly released
performance of *Rosenkavalier* — even though I
usually fade long before the curtain falls at
Lincoln Center. Then hot showers and a light
breakfast on the terrace, although September was
quickly disappearing and with it the warmth of an
early morning sun.

I re-enacted my lunch the day before with
Patricia Simmons. Desi was clearly interested,
although his only response when I reached the
dénouement — complete with its proposition and
sidewalk kiss — was to smile and murmur 'no
comment.'

'No comment!' I replied. 'The least you can
do is admit that you're flattered.'

'So why aren't you?' he asked, raising an

eyebrow infinitesimally.

'What I really want to know,' he continued, 'is whether she has another first-rate portrait tucked away in her apartment on the Upper West Side — or is everything modern there as well?'

'That I don't know, but I can certainly find out.'

'And did she give you permission to feature the Vigée Le Brun as part of your article?'

'You know, smart ass, you might just want to join me next time I interrogate her!'

'I don't think so, my dear. That might look like a *ménage* in the making, and I think that we had better hang fire on that possibility for the moment — as your friend Henry James used to say.'

'Poor Henry,' I replied. 'The Master was never even close to participating in a *ménage à trois* in his entire life — and probably not even in a *ménage à deux.*'

'And that, I imagine, is why he wrote about such things so powerfully: the mystery was part of the formula for him.'

'Time to leave your innocent novelists alone,' I said. 'Have any news?'

'Not as much as I would like. If you think of my model of triangulation, the situation seems to be something like this. When it comes to David's life in the Village, it appears that he wasn't intensely involved in the local gay scene.'

I must have put on a surprised look at this point, but Desi pressed on.

'The police have established the fact that he frequented a few bars, sometimes on his own, sometimes with a friend, but not that regularly. He was seen at some parties, but for the most part he seemed to stay at home and work — until, of course, he met Richard and began to have a more active social life.'

'Is there any evidence that he took the odd stranger back to his apartment?' I asked.

'He may well have done so; Sergeant Mullins thinks he has a lead or two. But logically speaking, that was something he was more likely to do before he met Richard, so I'm not sure whether that will go anywhere.

'As for the museum world, it seems that David was not very proficient at making enemies. I've spent some time with Stephen and Mullins, and so far it appears that David was either too nice or too junior a curator to antagonize his colleagues. He had a reputation both within the museum and beyond it for being intelligent, hard-working, and keeping his head down.

'But that,' Desi continued after a short pause, 'makes it all the more difficult to understand just why he was murdered. Unless, of course, there was some kind of back-scenes intrigue about the exhibition he was preparing.'

Desi ran his hand through his hair, a rare

indication of bafflement.

'On the other hand, he got along well with the conservators and preparators who were helping him with this Baroque painting show, and it looks as if he wrote enough of the catalogue and secured enough of the loans so that it will proceed.'

'So that leads us back to Sag Harbor and to our dinner *chez moi*. What have the police learned about Richard and Andy?'

'Well, it still doesn't look very good for Richard. He has stated that he didn't see David on the evening he was murdered, and so far the police have found no evidence to contradict that. But he really has no alibi. The telephone calls he made from his apartment that night were far enough apart so that it would have been possible for him to visit David and return in time to make the next call. And the records show that he did call David when he said he did.'

'And what about Andy?'

'Richard told the police that he didn't see Andy during the period in question. Andy corroborates Richard's statement, and he also seems to have an alibi for that Tuesday evening.'

'My God,' I said, 'just a little over a week ago.'

'Richard, you'll remember, was quite open about the fact that he and Andy had hit it off rather well that weekend. But he continues to maintain that David was only slightly irritated rather than highly jealous. And that's pretty much where things currently stand.'

'I don't know, Desi. You understand the museum world inside-out, but it just seems to me that something was going on there.'

'I'll keep my eyes peeled, but in the meantime I hope you don't mind, but I've made a date with your friend Renata. I've asked her to print out all of the photographs she took at your place that weekend. She's coming by for lunch tomorrow and we're going to sequence them together.'

'And what, exactly, are you looking for?'

'I honestly don't know at this point. But that's how all research essentially begins. If you know what you're going to find, then it's unlikely that you'll find anything else. But there's something else.'

'And what, exactly, is that?'

'I've hired a private investigator.'

'A private investigator? What in the world for?'

'Well, Abby, there are some things that the police clearly do very well, and then there are some things they simply do not have the time or the funding to cover.'

'Does Sergeant Mullins know what you're up to?' I asked.

'In principle.'

'And how did you find such a person?'

'"Such a person," my dear? That's really not quite fair. I assure you that Mr. Alphonse Lafargue —'

'Alphonse Lafargue?' I spluttered, barely able to control an explosion of mirth.

'I assure you that Mr. Alphonse Lafargue is rather more civilized than you imagine. He tells me that the days when private detectives stood under street lamps or combed through trash cans are pretty much over. Virtually everything is electronic these days — or, as he puts it, ninety percent the internet, ten percent shoe leather. When it comes to collating information about the people David associated with, he can save the police a lot of time.'

'And when will I have the pleasure of meeting Mr. Lafargue?'

'I'm not sure that you will, at least not yet.'

'And why not?' I asked suspiciously.

'Because you are obviously part of his investigation. You hosted the dinner, after all — '

'But Desi, you and I were together the night David was murdered!'

'Of course we were, but a complete investigation is just that. I naturally have my own hunches, but Mr. Lafargue needs to follow up on everything he can.

'Besides,' Desi added, 'John Hawes understands the rules.'

'What the fuck does this have to do with

John?' I asked, along with an excuse for my French.

'It's through John that I found the inimitable Mr. Lafargue. John has had to deal with some rather difficult clients over the years, and Mr. Lafargue has come in rather handy. And when I explained to John that his colleague would be taking a close look at all of us, he immediately agreed.

'In fact,' he added, with a laugh, 'he suggested that Mr. Lafargue might bring us some rather interesting information about his vivacious Dolores.'

'Oh God, Desi, I'm not sure that I like the feel of this. How discreet do you think he'll be?'

'In your case, dear, absolutely discreet. He won't be phoning your parents or interrogating your former lovers or itemizing your shoe bills, I assure you.'

'Thank God — especially about the shoe bills.'

'Speaking of which,' he said, 'I forgot to give you a little gift last night. We must have been interrupted by strangers.'

'Only two hundred of them, according to my rough count.'

He walked into the kitchen and soon returned with a beautifully wrapped box in his hands, just about the exact size of a shoe box, according to my well-practiced eye.

I carefully removed the handsome wrapping paper and soon had an extraordinary pair of plastic heels in my hands: black, of course, and just as tall as mother nature allows such things to grow.

'Oh, Desi,' I purred, 'you really shouldn't have. You've probably compromised your reputation in every sex and lingerie shop in Manhattan.'

'I'm afraid that my reputation was ruined in those establishments years ago — but not, of course,' he added, 'before I started pandering to you.'

'Spoiled once again,' I said. 'What's a girl to do?'

'Put them on, my dear. Simply put them on.'

And so I did, praying that the combination of inspired plastic and extreme elevation wouldn't bring me toppling to the terrace floor. And yet I found that I could strut my stuff rather nicely, especially once I had removed my bathrobe and made my way back to my generous benefactor.

'Come with me, Dr. Fairbrother. I have immoral longings in me, as Cleopatra didn't quite say.'

A quick tug at the terrycloth belt around his waist revealed sufficient evidence that another steamy episode might possibly be on his mind. It was certainly on mine.

An hour or so later we both had our marching orders. Desi was to proceed with his personal inquiries and I, for my part, was to see both young Jack Springer and Dennis and Madeleine on Thursday, as planned, but my intructions were to divulge only a bit of what Desi called 'undigested information' about the investigation in progress.

Thursday was also to bring me a few precious minutes at lunch with Renata, who confessed that she had enjoyed an interesting session with Desi.

'Sorry, Abby — sorry, sorry, sorry. Forget what I said a couple of weeks ago. I may never again say another word against Desmond.'

'And why not?' I countered. 'I have several I'd like to hurl at him myself from time to time.'

'Oh no, kiddo. It wasn't the weekend in Sag Harbor, lovely as it was. Nor that horrific cocktail party he gave two days ago.'

'So what, exactly, changed your mind?'

'It was looking at my photographs with him, actually. We must have looked at over a hundred of them yesterday, all of them fairly pedestrian to me. But not to him. He was so attentive to every detail. I feel flattered, I must admit. Nobody has ever looked so closely at my images before. Is he up to something?'

I wanted to tell her, rather melodramatically, that the solution to a murder might well hang in the balance. But instead I told her that it was typical of Desi, who didn't do anything by halves. Which was, after all, not too far from the truth.

'All I can say,' she continued, 'is that I found it intriguing to see him in action. Is this what he's like all the time?'

'No, thank God. He does have some down-time, although,' I quickly added with a rhetorical clearing of the throat, 'down-time may not actually be the best way to describe it.'

'Yes, Abby, I'm fully aware of your romantic exertions. But what about your latest admirer? I almost forgot about Jack. Was he as cocky as we had predicted?'

'Oh, very much so — just as well-muscled and long-lasting as a girl could wish. But he's not exactly my type, you know, even though I'm going to have a quick drink with him this evening.'

Or at least I think it's going to be a quick drink. We'll have to see. 'And what about Jeremy?' I asked in turn.

'So far, so good. He seems to be a genuinely nice person, so I'm hoping there won't be any unpleasant surprises along the way. But wish me luck anyway, old pal. I'll probably need it.'

After we had finished our thin-crust pizza with sun-dried tomatoes and goat cheese — 'Don't worry about the calories,' Renata told me as she ordered it; 'it contains all the basic food groups' — I headed home, read for two hours, took a long run along the East River, and then showered and began to change for the evening. I chose a red dress, black heels, and a black onyx necklace and earrings to match: something attractive but not *too* explicit, for I was going to meet Madeleine and Dennis for dinner later in the evening.

I met Jack at a little bar I'm quite fond of in an upscale hotel near my apartment. And by little I mean little: in London it would be called a snug-bar, with just enough room for a few people to stand, a few people to sit, and a bartender to anticipate your every need. It must be a survivor from the twenties or thirties, made all the more snug in those days, I imagine, by being completely saturated in smoke. It is, in every way, the perfect place to be indiscreet.

Jack appeared at seven-thirty wearing a black turtleneck and gray trousers — and smelling just as good as the week before. He had been persistent, I had been elusive, and we now eyed each other warily — and with pleasure. For someone who's definitely not my type, he certainly exuded all the right pheromones. And he seemed to know it.

I told him that he looked good. He told me that I looked great. I asked him about his teaching and his dissertation. He asked me about my essay and my book. I asked him whether he had seen Andy during the past week. He asked me whether I had seen Richard during the past week. It was as though we couldn't quite bring ourselves to mention David.

'Yes, I have,' he said, in answer to my question. 'Andy was devastated by the news of David's death. Or are we talking murder? He just couldn't figure it out.'

'Neither can we,' I said.

'Who's "we"?' he asked.

'Desmond. Richard. Me. Everyone we know, really.'

'So you've seen Richard?' he asked.

'Yes, he came over to Desmond's.'

'And how was he?'

'Terrible. He lost his lover, after all, and he seems to be the only plausible suspect in the case.'

'What do *you* think?' he asked.

'I don't think,' I answered. 'I have no head for this kind of thing. But Desmond is making his own inquiries as well as the police.'

'Desmond?' He sounded surprised.

'Yes. Not directly, mind you, but through various friends.'

He remained silent for a moment.

'I forgot to ask you, by the way,' I continued, 'whether the police had talked with Andy before you saw him.'

'Yes, they had. And it more or less freaked him out. It seems that Andy and Richard enjoyed themselves a bit too much together at your place, and David apparently became jealous.'

'Does Andy have an alibi?' I asked.

'I think so.'

'And you?' I asked — softly, hoping not to push too hard.

'Abby, I don't even know exactly when it happened.'

'Didn't the police talk with you?'

'No. Why should they?'

'Good point. Sorry. I guess I just think of the four of you together. But that was my party, not real life, right?'

'Well,' he answered, 'this is also real life, isn't it? Or am I missing something?'

'No, this is the real thing, you're right. And because it's the real thing it's also complicated.'

'It doesn't have to be,' he countered. 'I'm happy to be constrained by Abby's rules. I certainly was when we met last week.'

'At least you're direct, Jack — and that's one of the things I like about you. One of the many things I like about you.'

'Is dinner therefore in the cards?'

'Sorry, but no. I couldn't promise earlier, and as it turns out I'm having dinner with friends this evening. You remember Madeleine and Dennis?'

'Of course. But what about later?'

'Too late.'

'And what would a raincheck look like?'

'Something like this.'

I gave him a more-than-innocent kiss, paid

the bill, extricated myself from the snuggery, and hailed a nearby cab. It was time to move on, especially if I were not to keep Dennis and Madeleine waiting.

As it turned out, I had done just that — but I wasn't egregiously late and they are very old and very forgiving friends. I asked them to bring me up to speed on their architectural work — inside and out — and on the further escapades of their two Labradors, Butch and Lady Bird, who seem to think of Central Park as a mere extension of Sag Harbor. I, in turn, brought them up to date on my article for the shelter magazine and — more somberly — on the investigation into David's murder.

'Desmond has hired a private detective?' Madeleine cried. 'Does that mean that we're all under suspicion, Abby?'

'Not by the police,' I answered, quickly explaining Desi's process of triangulation and assuring them that his object was actually to free us of suspicion.

'But Abby,' Madeleine continued, 'neither Dennis nor I had ever clapped eyes on David Lundgren before we met him at your house two weeks ago.'

'And neither of us,' Dennis added, 'has ever been to Minneapolis in our entire lives!'

'Of course,' I answered, 'I fully understand, and so does Desmond. But the goal is to rule people out, and I'm sure that this private investigator with the fancy French name will do just that. I'm being researched as well, you know, even though I spent the night in question in the arms of our master detective.'

'Now that's some alibi,' Madeleine cooed. 'You must make Caesar's wife look downright suspect!'

After we had finished our Indian dinner, complete with three kinds of bread and very strong beer, I bade them goodbye and decided to walk my way home, even though it was a trek of fourteen or fifteen blocks. The evening was cool but not yet cold, and the lights in the windows of the shops along Second Avenue showed off their various wares to perfection. I like walking in the city just as much as I enjoy walking the beach on the Island: there's always something new to take in, and the sheer garishness of it all is somehow refreshing. How many nail salons, haircutters, drycleaners, and convenience stores can a single stretch of metropolitan pavement support, I often ask myself. How many delicatessens? How many overpriced food emporia? And how long will the little gems in this fragile equation — the authentically French patisserie, the Brazilian florist, the Czech seamstress who really does know how to make elegant alterations — continue to survive? At least for a while, I hoped; at least for a while.

I reached my building around eleven, tidied up the litter of papers in the outside lobby, let myself in, and walked upstairs to my apartment. As I turned the key in the second of my two locks, I suddenly realized that something was wrong. I felt a slight pressure on the door itself, and when I opened it a crack, I could feel a quiet rush of cold air escape from the darkened space within.

I immediately allowed the door to shut itself again, took off my shoes, and ran as quickly as I could down the hallway and then down the flight of stairs that led to the inner lobby. My heart was pounding furiously by this point, but no one was there — nor in the outer lobby, nor outside the building itself. I had to make a quick decision about what to do next. Should I stay put, or should I make a run for it along the length of the building and thus into the safety of the street? I chose the former, firmly pressing the building superintendent's buzzer as I fished for the cell-phone in my purse and began to dial Desi. No response from the super, but Desi — thank God — picked up his phone and was instantly decisive.

'Stay exactly where you are. If you hear any noise on the staircase, run outside as fast as you can. If you see anyone outside, retreat to the staircase. I'll be there in a few minutes — and so will the police.'

And so they were: first Desi, looking carefully

around the public side of the building before entering the lobby, and then two police officers whose siren I could hear as I buzzed Desi in. One officer planted himself outside, under my windows on the second floor, while Desi, the other policeman, and I walked upstairs and I turned the key in the lock a second time.

The apartment was dark even though I had left at least two lights on when I left. There was, however, no sign of anyone searching for anything: the drawers and closets had not been ransacked and — at first glance — nothing seemed to be missing. Whoever had entered the studio had climbed up the fire escape, neatly removed a pane of glass from one of the mullioned windows, which allowed the lock to be sprung and the bottom sash to be raised. Although I live on the second floor, I had never installed a security system, thinking that anyone who climbed up the side of the apartment building would easily be seen by the neighbors. Apparently I was wrong about that.

'Where do you keep your jewelry?' the officer asked.

I showed him a small but heavy safe tucked into one of my grandmother's old hat boxes. It was still locked and nothing was missing when I opened it.

'Where's your laptop?' Desi asked.

'On the writing desk,' I answered. But when I

followed his eyes in that direction, I immediately realized that the desk was bare.

'Any chance that you put it away?' Desi asked, putting his arms around me.

'No. It was right there.'

'Where do you keep your notes?'

'In a notebook in the desk.'

Desi opened the drawers. Everything was there except my small black notebook. But who would want my notebook?

'Have you backed your files up?' he asked.

My head was beginning to spin a little, but I managed to tell him — and the policeman — that all of my writing files were copied onto a memory stick.

'And where do you keep that?' the officer asked.

'In my Tampax dispenser.'

The policeman looked at me with what I took to be a mixture of discomfort and surprise. Desi looked at me with a mischievous smile. 'Congratulations, old girl,' he said, squeezing me affectionately. 'I doubt whether our intruder was as ingenious as you have been.'

And of course he was right. The *nouveau roman* was safely tucked away in an innocuous plastic tube, along with my thoughts about the essay I was about to write. The literary world could breathe a much-needed sigh of relief. Abigail Higginson would soon be back to work once again.

But first we had to decide what to do about the compromised apartment. Desi asked the police officer if someone could be hired to watch the building throughout the night. A quick phone call revealed that, for a few hundred dollars, a spare patrolman would soon be dispatched from the local station. With a sentry in place, the window could wait to be replaced until tomorrow — if the superintendent ever showed his face again.

Desi said that he would also arrange for his local security company to install an alarm system on Friday. In the meantime, I began to pack a bag so that I could spend the night in the carriage house.

'Abby,' Desi added, 'why don't you pack enough so that you can stay for a few days. Even with all of the precautions we're taking, I'd feel a lot more comfortable if you were safely with me through the weekend.'

'Okay. I'm much too tired to think straight this evening.'

And so, about twelve-thirty, we finally put ourselves in a cab and headed north. By the time we arrived, I was too tired to unpack, so I fell into bed and was quickly asleep.

Friday, 28 September

I was astonished to find that it was almost noon when I finally, slowly awakened. I soon learned that Desi had been up for several hours, arranging for various 'improvements' to my apartment, as he called them, and checking on me from time to time to see when I would once again join the land of the living.

I was also surprised to discover how refreshed I felt even before he brought me my first cup of coffee, a small dish of fruit, a silver bud vase with a fragrant rose in it, and an already digested copy of the *Times*. My sleep had been so deep and so long that the events of the previous evening seemed rather foggy — certainly not as threatening as they actually had been. But this *petit déjeuner*, petite as it was, soon brought a sense of reality home to me, and not just by perusing the newspaper.

Desi sat on the bed and poured me another cup of coffee. 'No need to rush, but Sergeant Mullins will be joining us at one o'clock. He's talked with the policemen on duty in your neighborhood last night, but we'll also have a chance to see if he knows any more.'

'And vice versa?' I asked.

'Precisely. I've had a long conversation with Mr. Lafargue this morning, who's been following up on a few of my hunches: life in the museum, David's friends, David's other interests. The results have been negative so far, but perhaps our detective sergeant can provide some missing information as well.'

'Are we having lunch?' I pertly asked. 'A girl can't live on a small bowl of fruit alone.'

'Well,' he conceded, 'there's no denying that. It will be ready by the time you're showered and dressed.'

And he was true to his word. Just as Sergeant Mullins arrived, I descended to the first floor to see that Desi had set the table on the terrace for three, with a medley of salads and a large pitcher of iced tea.

Officer Mullins was, I soon discovered, rather different from whatever stereotyped vision I had been entertaining in my somewhat addled brain. Far from being a hardboiled copper with strong Irish roots in the Bronx, he came across as a friendly pediatrician making an old-fashioned house call, complete with bifocals, rep tie, and a white button-down shirt. Even a quick glimpse at Desi's living room didn't seem to put him off as he shook my hand and followed us back to the terrace.

'Let's begin with the break-in to your apartment,' he began once we had seated ourselves at the table. 'Can you tell me, Ms. Higginson, what your day was like before you returned to your apartment?'

'Please, Sergeant, no one calls me Ms. except my mother. Abby is just fine. And yes, it was a busy day, now that I think back on it.'

Just *how* busy I didn't feel I had to explain in exquisite detail, but I laid out my 'movements' with some care and established a fairly precise time-line between the moment I left the carriage house and the early morning hour at which I unexpectedly returned to it.

'I'm interested,' Officer Mullins said, 'in the fact that during the day and evening you actually saw five of the eleven people who were at your house in Sag Harbor just a few days before David Lundgren's death. Was this something you planned?'

I turned to Desi, who smiled but said nothing.

'They're my friends, why shouldn't I see them?'

'Indeed,' he replied.

'But what does this have to do with the break-in?'

'Possibly nothing,' he answered. 'But it's important to know where various people were last night. I'm not concerned about your friend

Renata, but we're checking on the whereabouts of both Jack Springer and your friends the Hodgkinses.'

'Madeleine and Dennis!' I said. 'But I had just had dinner with them.'

'Of course,' he replied, 'but it's just as important to rule people out as it is to rule them in. In any case, there are several other people whom you know — and who knew David Lundgren — who need to be questioned as well, and we'll do that later today.'

'Other people who were at my party?' I asked.

'Yes, but a few additional people as well. We've identified at least two young men who accompanied David back to his apartment during the past year or so, and I'm also keeping an eye on a few of his colleagues at the museum.

'What intrigues me about the break-in last night, however,' he continued, 'is what the police report says the prowler took with him — or her. According to the report, there were only three items of value in your studio: your computer, your art work, and your jewelry. The jewels were well hidden, and either the thief wasn't interested in searching for them or he ran out of time just as you arrived. The prints would have been cumbersome to steal. If, however, he was only interested in what could easily be removed and fenced, then there is no reason why he would have taken your notebook as well as your computer. And this suggests to me that he was really interested in retrieving anything that might have contained your thinking — and possibly Dr. Fairbrother's thinking — about the murder.'

'Quite possibly,' Desi said, speaking up for the first time. 'But there's an alternative as well, Sergeant, which is that whoever entered Abby's apartment wanted to make her feel vulnerable. It may have been immaterial what was taken. Other than, as a writer, one of the things she would be bound to miss most is her work.'

'Who among your acquaintances would understand this about you?' Mullins quickly responded.

'You mean Andy Cameron?' I blurted out without thinking. Of the group at Sag Harbor, he was the one who had harped on about literature and had made it quite clear that he was interested in my work as a novelist. 'I thought that he had a solid alibi for the night of the murder.'

'I'm talking to you about last night. As for earlier, yes, he seems to have an alibi,' the sergeant replied, 'but all three young men — Richard, Jack, and Andy — were very much in David Lundgren's orbit by the end of that weekend. I can't say anything about Jack Springer at this point — nor can I say much about the two men with whom David had trysts in the Village. Based on my talk with Richard, David's boyfriend seems to have hit it off with Andy to the point where David was uncomfortable, if not downright jealous. And that necessarily placed Andy and David in an adversarial relationship as well, even though they barely knew each other.'

'Sergeant,' Desi asked, 'have you been able to establish whether anything was stolen from David's apartment?'

'The only person who can help us with that is Richard, who was there several times during the past few months. Richard tells us that everything seems to be there: a small television set, a stereo, David's clothing, a few things hanging on the wall. It's a small apartment, believe me.'

'What about a computer?' Desi asked. 'Did David own a laptop, or did he have one that belonged to the Met?'

'I'll ask the museum,' Officer Mullins replied, 'but there certainly isn't one in the apartment, and there isn't one in his office, which has a standard pc with an oversized screen. And I don't believe that Richard mentioned one either.'

'Sergeant,' Desi continued, 'have your colleagues taken a close look by now at all of the files on David's computer?'

'Yes, they have; nothing surprising.'

'Do you mind my asking, are there any online auction records on the computer?' Desi continued.

'Nothing mentioned in the report. Is there a reason you ask?'

'No, not particularly.'

'Well, thank you for your time. I'll stay in touch regarding the break-in. Perhaps I should take a note of your cell number, Dr. Fairbrother?'

I gave Desi a sympathetic smile as he politely — but, as I well knew, quite reluctantly — reached into his wallet and fished out his mobile number, a number so little used that he can never remember what it is.

After the avuncular Sergeant Mullins had left — without touching his lovely bone-china plate, I sadly noted — I sat down with Desi once again and started to pick his brain.

'Something's on your mind,' I told him. 'What's up?'

'Two things. First, David must have had a laptop, whether he owned one himself or whether the museum did. How else could he have worked at home so many evenings rather than hanging out like everyone else in the Village?'

'And the second thing, Sherlock?'

'Is just as obvious as the first. Those who knew David at all knew that he was a collector, at least in a modest way. Do you remember what he said at your dinner party? Jack said something rather belligerent about collecting, but David happily confessed that he was a collector to the extent that he could afford to be so.'

'And so the moral is . . . ?'

'Virtually anyone who collects on a modest scale follows the online auctions, even if they can't always participate in them. And I very much doubt whether David would have been an exception, although I can't remember him mentioning any specific purchases to me. In any case, if his office computer doesn't reveal this kind of history, a laptop surely would. And I'm quite curious to know just how extensive his online collecting was.'

'But what if there was no laptop?' I asked.

'I'm certain there was.'

'And what if the laptop is therefore missing? And what could that have to do with my laptop being stolen?'

'David's missing laptop presents problems, but not insurmountable ones. And it also,' he added, 'suggests some intriguing new directions of inquiry.

'But let's return to this later, Abby,' he continued. 'I think it's time to pay a visit to your crimson-colored hideaway and make sure that our contractors have kept their part of the bargain. And then I suggest that we go to a film or to the theater, something that will focus our minds on something else.'

'Good plan,' I replied. 'Let me freshen up and away we go.'

Abigail's cocoon, it turned out, had been the focus of attention for a considerable number of people during the past twelve hours or so. The police had been over my apartment with their proverbial fine-tooth comb, searching for fingerprints, footprints, and the odd morsel of DNA.

Then, later in the morning, the superintendent had replaced the small missing pane of glass in my beautifully mullioned window while Desi's security firm installed a simple system connected to my land line (which I had actually considered relinquishing just a month earlier). And then, bless his heart, my somewhat embarrassed super — 'I am so sorry! I am almost always here late at night, Miss Abby' — had coaxed his wife into cleaning up after the police, the security installation expert, and her husband. All Desi and I had to do was rearrange the furniture, straighten the prints, and make sure that my clothing was more or less in order, including all those dresses, heels, and thongs that we hadn't moved over to the carriage house. By the time we were done, my little *pied à terre* had never looked better.

But that still didn't mean that I was going to stay there anytime soon. 'Abby, why don't you stay at the carriage house tonight. I have tickets for the fall antiques show on Saturday, by the way; would you like to go?'

'Could we invite John and Dolores as well?' I asked. 'I hardly had a chance to wave at them during your party this week.'

'Very nice idea, darling. And then perhaps we can give them a quiet dinner afterwards, unless they already have other plans.'

But they didn't, and for a moment the weekend looked as if it would be as pleasant as it could be under the circumstances. But then came Sergeant Mullins's call, just as we were returning to the carriage house to change for the evening. I've rarely seen Desi work from his cellphone, let alone take notes while standing in the kitchen.

'And what,' I immediately asked once he'd finished, 'did you learn from Sergeant Mullins?'

'Quite a bit, Abby: some of it expected, some of it not.'

'So we were right in assuming that David had a laptop at his apartment?'

'Almost certainly so,' Desi answered. 'The museum had loaned him one so that he could work at home while he prepared his exhibition. The laptop wasn't in his office — and it wasn't in his studio — so it's almost certain that whoever killed him took it with him.'

'Why would they do that?'

'That's what we need to find out.'

Desi was visibly processing what he'd learned, so I hesitated to interrupt.

'Mullins has gone back through the records on David's computer at the museum, and it appears there is no evidence that he was participating in auctions online.'

'And why, precisely, is that so important?'

'Because it suggests that David was using

another account for his personal affairs.'

'And so what was unexpected?'

'Richard told us, less than a week ago, that he didn't visit David on the night of the murder — that he was in fact working at his own apartment, although he also made a few phone calls.

'It turns out,' Desi continued, 'that Mullins has been working very hard to check out Richard's alibi, and earlier this afternoon he finally hit pay dirt.'

'Pay dirt?' I asked. 'My goodness, you really are becoming involved in this business!'

'They were able to trace a taxi driver who has testified that he dropped Richard off very near David's apartment on Tuesday. He can't provide an exact time, but it was roughly when David was killed.'

'Oh God, Desi,' I muttered. 'Does that completely destroy Richard's alibi?'

'Well, it certainly means that he was lying both to the police and then to us. And although it doesn't mean that Richard necessarily killed his friend, it does seem to suggest that he visited David, that he had enough time to see him and return to his own apartment — and that, for whatever reason, he's been covering his tracks ever since.'

'Do you think that we should talk with him again?'

'Mullins will pull him in for questioning now.

I imagine that, whether or not Richard is indeed guilty of this crime, he's going to be one very frightened young man.'

'Obviously, I don't know him well at all, but he certainly doesn't seem capable of murdering someone — or even of breaking and entering.'

'Frightened people often do desperate and highly unpredictable things, Abby.'

'I imagine so. What does my poet say? "Perhaps my semblance might deceive the truth." And I suppose that it often does.'

'Nicely put, both by you and by your blind regicide.'

'That's the great thing about the sonnet form. Language under extreme pressure, as one of my teachers liked to phrase it.'

'And murder no doubt does much the same thing?' Desi asked.

'Does what?' I replied.

'Murders are presumably committed by people under extreme pressure, but the fact of murder places everyone within its circuit under intense pressure as well. Even those who are innocent, if that's the case with Richard Yung.'

'Well, I certainly hope that he is.'

'And if he is, what's the alternative?' he responded.

'I guess I'd prefer not to think about that.'

'Well, my dear, I'm afraid that we have no choice but to think about it. And, if possible, to do something about it as well.'

But for now, we decided to sally forth to our large local cineplex on Third Avenue, where, in the raucous anonymity of another two hundred souls, we laughed our way through the latest installment of the much-extended adventures of Commander James Bond. Not that we were supposed to laugh, of course, but somehow Mr. Fleming's sense of high sophistication — social, sexual, and automotive — had long ago become high camp. The only way not to wince one's way through it was to howl in all the wrong places and dig our respective elbows into each other.

When we were comfortably seated at our favorite bistro afterwards, feeling a little embarrassed at my choice for our last-minute evening's entertainment, I apologized to Desi for the mindlessness of it all.

'Don't apologize,' he replied. 'There's nothing wrong with mass entertainment if it's done well enough. After all, *Gone with the Wind* is first-rate trash, and there should always be a place for such things, don't you think?'

'Frankly, my dear, I don't give a damn about *Gone with the Wind*,' I replied. 'It's just a shame that all of the real glamour of the original books has been completely eviscerated in the films.'

'I must confess that I haven't read any of them.'

'Well, you should take one to the beach next

time. 007 is actually a borderline incompetent. And a not-very-secret secret agent. He's very good at smoking, driving, and drinking, but he's a second-rate gambler whose every move places either himself or his damsel in distress. And eventually both of them!'

'Hmm,' Desi replied. 'I can't wait to pick one up.'

'The bad guys are much more accomplished than our man in his bespoke suit and Aston Martin or supercharged Bentley. Rather like Dickens, come to think of it.'

'As I said, I can't wait to pick one up.'

'We need to take both you and your book to a nearby beach fairly soon. I'd love to change the scenery just a little. I think it would be good for both of us.'

'I absolutely agree with you, but I think we should stay close by, at least for the moment. And you should stay at the fortress as much as possible.'

'And just how safe is the fortress?' I asked.

'As safe as houses, as the English used to say. The entire place is on a fairly sophisticated security system, and the police station is around the corner. So I think that we're covered there.'

'So what shall we cook for John and Dolores tomorrow? Beefsteak for him and spicy Latin fare for her?'

'I'm sure we can do better than that.

Whatever we do, we'll have to prepare it ahead of time and have it more or less ready to serve. So my usual suspects would be *osso buco*, a *boeuf Bourguignon*, a *ragu bolognese*, or something that could be marinated and quickly grilled. Unless, of course, it's pouring outside.'

'But you have an indoor grill, Desi. In fact, you have an indoor everything, *caro ricco*.'

'But it's always better grilled outside, unless it's something that's easily scorched, like pork or lamb chops. What's the forecast, milady?'

'I have absolutely no idea. I never do, as you well know.'

'Well, let's plan for the worst and prepare something for indoors ahead of time. You get to choose: Italian, French, or Italian?'

'Indian.'

'That's not an option.'

'It certainly is. You've got all the spices, and you've also got that fabulous slow-cooker hidden away in your lower cabinets. We could cook chicken or lamb or pork in it quite easily and have it ready when we return.'

'Are you willing to take responsibility?' he asked.

'As long as I've got a decent *sous-chef,* someone hard-working and very pliant.'

'It sounds as if you want a servant or a slave, not a *sous chef,* my dear.'

'A servant in the kitchen, a slave in the

bedroom. Do we have a deal?'

Indeed we did, but we were both tired when we returned to the carriage house, taking a quick bath together, sipping Pellegrino instead of champagne, and slipping under Desi's crisp linen sheets well before midnight.

Saturday, 29 September

Daybreak was another matter, however. I read somewhere that the male of the species experiences his highest testosterone level first thing in the morning, and it is certainly true of the lord of this particular manor. He can be very demanding, in the best possible way — you don't need an entire pot of coffee and four sections of the newspaper to convince you that the day has begun in earnest.

I enjoy our little cat-and-mouse game of who's going to get what first, and I'm pretty good at buying enough time to drink a decent cup of coffee and make a stately trip to the bathroom.

But not on this Saturday morning. My unkempt and unshaven Adonis decided that all of the niceties of civilized behavior could wait. Given the fact that I usually sleep in nothing more than a mask, my defenses were necessarily weak. I begged for coffee — to no avail. I begged for mercy — to no avail. I tried tickling him in various places, won a momentary respite, and hightailed it to the bathroom as quickly as I could.

Desi was amused but still determined when he politely entered a few minutes later. By this time I had put on my new pair of plastic heels and had a plan up my sleeve — or would have had a plan up my sleeve if I were actually wearing a sleeve in which to place it.

'Look, darling,' I fake whined. 'I'm not going to be of much use to you unless I've had a cup of coffee, and you're not going to be of much use to me unless you shave and shower.'

'Both of your points are arguable,' he replied.

'So,' I continued, 'I'll make you a deal. You make us some coffee, I'll make the bed, and then I'll give you a shave in the shower. I've always wanted to play with that blond stubble of yours.

'Do we have a deal?' I asked.

'It depends on what follows.'

'If you bring me two cups of coffee, anything your heart desires.'

'It's not my heart you're squeezing, my dear.'

I must confess that I haven't had so much fun in a long, long time — or at least not in a shower. Desi turned out to be a rather squeamish subject as I ministered to him as carefully as I could, making sure that his sideburns were even and that I concluded the process by shaving his cheeks and neck both up as well as down.

And then once we had finally satisfied my closely shaven Adonis's *other* needs and taken a proper shower, we began to plan the rest of our day. A trip to the local food emporium, my preparation of dinner while Desi rustled up a decent lunch, and then a long, leisurely walk north along the river and back, eventually landing us at the Armory on Park Avenue, where we would meet John and Dolores around six.

The Armory stages antiques shows twice a year. This one is not quite as fancy as the exhibition in the winter, but I love it because there are often a few items that even I might be able to afford – not that I ever buy anything, but I enjoy thinking that I could.

As I saw Dolores enter the lobby, I took her in in all of her larger-than-life glory. She was sporting a white silk blouse, silver trousers, and a pair of high heels in a beautiful dark purple that reflected one of the colors in the small scarf she had tied to her handbag. Nothing could have been more sleek or tasteful, and yet she seemed — well, I'll just say it — garish.

Was it her hair? Her makeup? Her jewelry? No, I told myself, it was that powerful combination of hip and breast, neither of which could be entirely contained. She knew how to move, and she enjoyed making a splash. And thus with Dolores — as with John, for that matter — it was always anchors away.

And so we launched ourselves arm-in-arm down the central aisle of the show while Desi and

John made their own way from booth to booth. There was a riot of color and shape and texture: furniture on antique carpets, paintings and drawings hung on richly papered walls, and a *mélange* of decorative objects ranging from Meissen and Imari to Inuit and Hopi. No matter how bad the weather, no matter how bad the economy, when you come here, all is right with the world.

'Oh, Dolores, come look!' I was tempted by one item: a small maritime etching by Winslow Homer. It would look quite at home in my crimson cocoon, I thought, mixing nicely with the other black-and-white prints there. I chatted with the dealer, took his card, and eventually tore the two of us away to find John and Desi, who were studying a beautiful small painting of house-tops in what looked to be a sun-dappled Italian city.

'Naples, to be precise,' Desi informed me. 'A lovely example of Thomas Jones' work at its very best. I much prefer these urban landscapes to his more pastoral images, lovely as those also are.'

John was eyeing the painting just as carefully, but he remained enigmatically silent until we all stepped out into the aisle again and made our way towards the bar at the back of the hall.

'It's perfect, Desmond — and perfect for you,' he then said with his air of sonorous certainty.

'But it's over-priced. I know the dealer fairly well, and if you're interested I can follow through once the fair is over.'

'That's kind of you, John,' Desi answered.

'But what if the painting is sold before the show is over?' Dolores asked.

'That,' Desi quickly answered, 'is the risk one takes. If I had to have it at any cost, I would negotiate on the spot and then carry it home under my arm. But desires as well as works of art have their individual price tags, and the price I've set on this particular desire is a bit lower than the one attached to this particular painting.'

Dolores smiled broadly and happily accepted the glass of champagne John offered her. We were halfway through the show, and I wondered whether John himself had seen anything that tempted him.

'Visually, yes, but financially, no. If I bought for myself, I'd feel that I had overpaid, and if I bought for my clients, I'd have a hard time selling at an even higher price. So, like Desmond, I'll play the waiting game and see what happens to some of the better pictures in the next few months.'

'And you, Dolores?' Desi asked.

'Beautiful Greek boys.'

'Which ones?' I asked. 'There are so many,' I added a bit facetiously.

'Aisle on the right, fourth booth from the front. Always the same dealer, always fabulous objects,' Dolores answered.

Desi and I stole a quick look at each other.

'And which one do you fancy this time, darling?' John asked her. 'Marble, terracotta, or stone?'

'Marble this time: probably Hellenistic, although I didn't have a chance to talk to the dealer.'

'And the price?' John asked.

'He never puts a price on them, silly. You'll have to negotiate on my behalf.'

'It's more likely,' John added, 'that I'll have to sell a picture first! But come, let's take a proper look at it. Excuse us for a moment, dear friends.'

Off they sallied, sleek and confident and full of good cheer.

'My oh my,' I cooed in Desi's ear. 'Surprises never cease.'

'You're right, my dear. I had no idea that she collected — and had I known, I would have guessed that she had an eye for the decorative arts, something showy and dramatic, something that would match her work in the theater.'

'Well,' I added, 'while we have a moment to ourselves, why don't you take a quick look at the Homer I'm rather interested in. I wonder whether it might pass Dr. Fairbrother's inspection.'

Indeed it did. Desi carefully made his way to the booth without me, looked at everything on offer, and then asked for the price of three prints, the Homer among them. When he returned, he simply nodded in agreement and then asked me whether I wanted to buy it now or take a slight risk and purchase it after the show had ended.

I decided that the price Desi had been quoted was reasonable enough — and adding something new to my metropolitan lair would make good psychological sense just at the moment, even if I would ask Desi to take good care of it until I returned for good to said lair. So we returned to the dealer, cemented the deal at what turned out to be a price a fraction lower still, and happily placed my small treasure under Desi's arm.

By the time John and Dolores appeared in the far aisle, we were ready to head on home.

Neither of them was carrying a small Greek head under *their* arms, I noticed, but when we were out on the street again, I learned that the boy in question was being shipped to John's weekend cottage in Connecticut.

'John's such a sweetheart,' Dolores said. 'I'll have to do something very special for him in return.'

I had no difficulty in imagining just how well she would fulfill her end of the bargain.

A few minutes later we climbed into a taxi and headed towards the carriage house. A medley of appetizers awaited us, and Desi poured out glasses of wonderfully crisp Sancerre while I checked on the main dish in the slow-cooker. Before coming to the table, like a magician, Desi turned down the lights, turned on the music to low, and took a match to a series of candles on our table. Presto: the scene was set for an intimate dinner *pour quatre*.

'Oh, Desmond,' she crooned, 'you should have been a set designer.'

'Tut tut, my darling,' John added. 'He *is* a set designer, except that in Desmond's case he just happens to own the entire set!'

'Nicely put,' I chimed in. 'Now what would you like to follow your Sancerre: beer (Desmond has some of that wonderful Indian stuff) or a slightly sweet Riesling?'

Beer for John, Riesling for the rest of us as Desi took everyone's order and returned to the kitchen.

'Really, Abby,' Dolores whispered before he returned, 'why in the world don't you want to live here?'

'That,' I firmly replied, 'is the subject of another conversation. Not here, and not now! But you can take me to lunch some day and try to tease the answer out of me.'

'It's a deal,' she replied.

When Desi returned and we had made our way through both the curried chicken and the current art market, the conversation finally turned to David and to the ensuing investigation. Both John and Dolores knew very little beyond what Desi had told them over the phone some time ago, so it was time to bring everyone up to date.

'Triangulation,' Dolores murmured after Desi described his method for trying to work through the little evidence he had.

'I don't like that word, Desmond. It reminds me too much of strangulation.'

'Or evisceration,' John helpfully added.

'Well, for what it's worth, Dolores, one thing we do know is that poor David wasn't strangled,' Desi explained. 'According to the police, it was a blow to the head. It appears that he was in a struggle with someone and was thrown to the floor, where he hit his head on a hard object, apparently the hearth of the fireplace. Death was probably instantaneous.'

'How grisly,' John muttered.

'Death usually is,' Desi continued, 'not to mention murder. In any case, the supposition is that David let someone into his apartment, a struggle ensued, and his visitor then left with David's laptop in his possession.'

'Unless, of course,' I added, 'someone else visited the scene after David had been killed and took the computer at that point.'

'And how probable,' Desi replied, but with a smile, 'do you think that is? David's death and the disappearance of the laptop surely have to be linked.'

'But if it's now looking likely that Richard did drop by the apartment, he could have taken the laptop to see if he could figure out what David had got himself into. He could have lied about it to avoid being under suspicion.'

'But how do we know that Richard went to the apartment?' John quickly asked.

'Short answer, we can't be a hundred percent certain,' Desi continued, ' but the one single fact the police have been able to establish is this: that even though Richard stated that he had not seen David that evening, he was in fact dropped off by a taxi not far from David's apartment at roughly the hour in question. Richard is being questioned again, but assuming (as I do) that Richard did visit David, he either did so before or after someone murdered his lover, or he killed David himself.'

'Did Richard have a key to David's apartment? Was there any sign of forced entry?' Dolores asked.

'He told the police that he did not — but he's already lied. It would be virtually impossible, in any case, to prove that such a key existed.'

'What about Monsieur Lafargue? Has he come up with anything so far?' John asked.

'Nothing concrete.'

'So does that mean that none of us is under suspicion, you mean?' John added.

'Precisely. So far your friend has been able to find no prior link between David and the two of you, Renata, Jeremy Lipkin, Madeleine and

Dennis Hodgkins, Jack Springer, or Andy Cameron beyond the fact, of course, that we were all together in Sag Harbor the weekend before David died. And as for Richard, Abby, and myself, there is no evidence that points to any issues with David apart from some possible jealousy that David may have experienced once he and Richard met Andy that weekend.'

'But why, Desmond,' Dolores asked, 'would we be investigated in the first place?'

'Because I want to prove to the police incontrovertibly that with the exception of the three of us, none of our guests that weekend had a previous relationship with David. What the police need to focus on is what may have been going on at the museum or in the gay community, where he may have been well-known. This is where they might find people who can shed some light.'

Desi was thoroughly into his subject now, and had even started to pace in front of the glowing fire.

'There's also a hunch, and perhaps no more than that, but as a collector and scholar I've always paid close attention to such things. Call it intuition in this case, but as Abby will testify, both of us sensed that David was unusually quiet throughout most of our evening together. Not during lunch or on the beach. But later, and especially as the evening drew on, he appeared — to me at least — to be holding himself in.'

'But wouldn't that be explained by what Richard has told you?' Dolores asked. 'By the fact that David was upset because Richard and Andy seemed attracted to each other?'

'It certainly could be — and that's one line of argument our colleagues in the police department are currently following, although they're interested in other issues as well.'

'But you're not convinced, are you, Desmond?' I asked.

'Not yet. I just feel that there is more to this. And that's possibly where Lafargue will make the difference. In the meantime, I'm more or less stymied.'

'Although,' Desi continued after a short pause, 'I do have a glimmer of an idea about how to find out more.'

'And what's that?' John asked.

'Would you,' Desi asked as he eyed each of us seriously for a moment, 'agree to join me for a re-enactment of the dinner Abby hosted in Sag Harbor?'

'Darling Desmond, how in the world can you re-enact a dinner party?' Dolores immediately asked, laughing uncomfortably.

'Not a bad question,' I added, not liking where this was going.

'Perhaps re-enactment is the wrong word, then. What I have in mind is simply this. Would you join me for dinner, here in the carriage house, at

190

which all of the other members of Abby's party would join us?'

'Of course we would,' John said.

'But would we be safe?' Dolores asked.

'Yes, you would be safe,' Desi replied. 'On my honor.'

'Then I'm happy to join you, Desmond,' Dolores replied. 'It actually sounds very theatrical, don't you think, Abby?'

'Very theatrical,' I responded, as a small sliver of dread began to creep across my chest. What was Desi up to?

Once John and Dolores had finished a simple dessert of macerated (and slightly intoxicated) fruit, we saw them to the door and gave them departing hugs and kisses.

'They are certainly an entertaining couple,' I mused as we gathered the remaining dishes and made our way back to the kitchen. 'What I especially like about them is their refusal to take each other entirely seriously.'

'Which is a rather enlightened form of accommodation, don't you think?' Desi added.

'Absolutely,' I replied. 'And what do you think they are saying about us?'

'I wouldn't be surprised if they were saying exactly the same thing.'

'Does that mean, Dr. Fairbrother, that there is the slightest possibility that you don't take Miss Abigail Higginson, blue-stocking author and scourge of New England mores, entirely seriously?'

No answer to that one. Just a warm kiss as Desi lifted me into his arms and slowly carried me upstairs, where a late-night bath and an inviting bed awaited me.

Sunday – Tuesday,
30 September-2 October

On Sunday I slept in once again, blissfully unaware of the information Desi was receiving and the instructions he was dispatching in the kitchen below. There was no one, this time 'round, to check on my well-being or to bring me coffee on a sterling-silver breakfast tray. Or ten sections of the *Times*. Spoiled brat that I was – or at least pretended to be – I put on my robe and made my way from the bedroom to the bathroom, then downstairs to the kitchen, then through the French doors that open onto the terrace, where I found Desi sitting quietly in the mid-morning sun, attired in his black swimsuit and the remnants of his white cotton bathrobe, which had fallen onto the back of his chair. His eyes were closed, and it took him a moment to sense that I was there.

'Sorry, Abby!' he exclaimed. 'I've been inattentive. Let me run inside and find you a cup of coffee.'

As he did so, I moved one of the other garden chairs next to his and judged that I, too, could indulge in some baring of the flesh on such a beautiful morning. We don't enjoy all of the privacy that the pool in back of Captain Logan's house affords, but it's better than no privacy at all — and so far the neighbors have not filed any official complaints with our local precinct.

'What a lovely morning,' I said when he returned. 'And I seriously overslept. Perhaps it was one way to escape this sense of dread I'm feeling about the dinner party you've proposed. I suppose it's partly the discomfort of seeing everyone together again, and partly not liking to feel more than a bit in the dark.'

'Well, my dear, if you had appeared an hour or so ago, I would have given you a reassuring pat on the back and told you that the dinner might never take place. But the telephone lines have been busy since then, and I now have more information from Lafargue. Not everything I was hoping for — and I still need to talk to the Inspector and to Richard — but I at least have my central suspicion . . .' He hesitated a moment. 'I won't say confirmed, but at least put actively in play.'

'Are you going to share your suspicion with me?'

'That's what I've been thinking about.'

'And what's your verdict?' I asked.

'My inclination — my strong inclination at this point — is not to, at least for now. I may be wrong in my suspicions, after all. But if I'm right,' he continued, 'I don't want to put you in a difficult position. I will very much need your help with this dinner, and I want you to be absolutely yourself. You're friends with all of the people who will sit at our table, and I want you to behave as you normally would, extending your hospitality to everyone who arrives.

'I have a feeling,' he added, 'that no one will want to join us. Not even John and Dolores. So by keeping you a bit in the dark, I'm hoping to make the best of a very difficult situation.'

'My God, Desi, it all sounds rather cloak and dagger. Of course I'll help, but is something bad going to happen? How soon will we need to engage the caterers and security?' I attempted to make light of it, but my mind was in a spin thinking about what Desi was going to orchestrate.

'Thanks for being a good sport, Abby. But I really don't think that security will be in order, although the right crew of waiters certainly will.'

Sunday and Monday were very strange indeed. Normally I'm the one who's inconveniently on the phone — either the cell or the landline — but whenever I looked up there was Desi on another call. It was very uncharacteristic of him, to say the least, and yet he seemed to be completely oblivious, such was the intensity of those extended conversations. First it was Mullins, then

Lafargue, then Mullins again, then many more chats with our French Canadian detective. When would it come to a passable conclusion?

Soon enough, it turned out.

I had returned from my run along the river on late Monday afternoon and had taken a long, hot shower. I put on what I consider to be my casual-sexy best for a quiet night at home in the big city: one of those tight string-body tops (in white), a pair of black silk trousers, tapered at the ankle, and some strappy red heels. Oh — and a small ladybug brooch near my collar bone.

But when I joined Desi in the kitchen, he was still on the telephone, jotting down notes once again, and motioning me to take something cold from the freezer. And so I did, mixing ice-cold vodka with some Lillet blanc and the tiniest touch of orange liqueur — what one of my favorite bartenders calls a French kiss. After properly bruising this concoction with ice in a shaker, I poured the liquid ambrosia into two antique flutes, added an ice cube to each glass, and topped both drinks off with a twist of orange.

Desi soon hung up the phone, took a quick sip, made a slight purring noise, and then gave me a loving kiss.

'Desmond,' I said.

'Desmond?' he replied.

'Desmond,' I said, 'will you please do me a small favor? I have a sense that we're about to shift into campaign mode, and if that's the case, I'd like you to take a nice shower, change into something truly comfortable, and then tell me what the hell's going on while I slave over supper in the kitchen. Do we have a deal?'

'You're right: I'm as tight as a knot and need to stretch. I'll be a new man in twenty minutes or so.'

'I don't want a new man, darling. Just a Desi rather than a Desmond.'

'Point taken. Off I go, leaving most of your lovely drink in the fridge.'

When he returned he looked noticeably more at ease, dressed in a black turtleneck, a pair of much-loved chinos, and some cashmere slippers that were already making their autumnal debut together with the to-be-expected change of scent. In the winter it's usually a strong pairing of coriander and civet — or what passes for civet these days. In the spring it's a lovely citrus concoction with grapefruit notes. In the summer it's a lighter citrus with lemon or cedrat. And in the autumn it's an interesting combination of lavender, vanilla, and musk — not overpowering by any means, but my first encounter with it in late September is always a wake-up call.

'Mmm, you certainly smell good — and you don't look so bad, either. Perhaps dinner will have to be put on hold for an hour or so.'

'Oh no, my dear. We have a bargain. I'll just

rescue my drink, then I can fill you in while you perform your culinary magic.'

'Magic, schmagic,' I replied. 'It's called slicing, chopping, and dicing, and a girl could use a little help from time to time.

'But not this time, you'll be pleased to learn,' I added. 'We're actually in very good shape. I've made us a light Provençal fish stew and a fresh baguette, together with a salad of peppers, olives, sun-dried tomatoes, and my famously frantic lettuce.'

'Sounds delicious. What are we going to have to drink?' he asked.

'I couldn't find any bottles of rosé in the wine chiller, but I did find a bottle of Gavi di Gavi in your cellar. Will that pass muster?'

'Perfect. But in the meantime, let me outline the plan of action. Are you ready?'

'Fire away,' I replied. 'You can have a second French kiss if you need it.'

'I probably will. In the meantime, here's roughly where we stand. I've had conversations with both Lafargue and Mullins, and Mullins seems to be comfortable with my plan so far. I also think that I have most of the information I need to launch our dinner later this week. Renata has sent me digital files of her photographic work in Sag Harbor and I'll spend part of tomorrow editing them. I've lined up the catering for Wednesday evening. I've extended invitations to our weekend guests to join us then . . .'

'But will they all do so?' I quickly asked.

'Rather surprisingly, they will. They seem to want to see a resolution just as much as we do. No problem, of course, with Dennis and Madeleine, nor with Jeremy and Renata, nor with John and Dolores. I talked with Richard briefly today while you were out and he will come. So will Jack Springer.'

'You've already asked him?'

'Yes. I thought that the invitation should come from me. With all three of our young friends I'm simply asking them to join me in helping to solve David's murder.'

'Simply asking them?'

'Well, of course not, but I'm trying to keep the context as positive as I can, even if it's a necessary fiction.'

'What about Andy Cameron?'

'I haven't been able to reach him yet, and — as you well know — I don't like to leave messages. Especially under the circumstances. I'll try again this evening.'

'And what about the police? Where do they fit in?'

'They'll be in the background, Abby. Close enough, but not in plain sight.'

'Oh God, Desi, this sounds complicated — and dangerous.'

'I don't think that it will be either, my dear.

Think of it as another discussion around the dinner table, only this time we'll be playing a different game.'

'So you believe that it was either Richard, Andy, or Jack who was involved?'

I shuddered at the thought that Jack might have had something to do with David's death, and not just because of our steamy evening together.

Desi quickly put his arms around me, gave me a gentle hug, and moved us in the direction of the stove. It was a relief to be able to concentrate on something as innocent as nervous lettuce and a spicy fish stew.

On Tuesday morning, at breakfast, I asked Desi whether the date for our dreaded dinner was still fixed.

'Yes, my dear, it's still set for tomorrow evening — unless, of course, Andy can't join us, but I'm imagining that he will if we can be in touch with him, given the persuasion of yours truly, to say nothing of the police. But I still need to talk with him.'

'All right,' I responded, 'D-Day and counting. Thirty-six hours to go. How can I help?'

'It's fine, Abby. Leave me to sort everything out. Why don't you focus on writing your essay? The time I'll need your insight will be on the night itself.'

'Well, yes, I do need to get on with it. I'll give Patricia Simmons a call. There are a couple of facts I need to check. Perhaps I should ask her over for an evening *intime*.'

'Abby, my sweet. We should all have healthy ambitions for exploration— roads not yet taken, as one of your curmudgeonly poets once said — but I suggest that we shelve this one for the season.'

'Party pooper,' I replied.

'Abby, I love you dearly . . .'

'Oh my God: the "L" word, no less.'

'But I propose a time-out on anything remotely adventurous in that direction, with all of our energies geared towards our ordeal tomorrow evening.'

'Party pooper,' I repeated, but as I did so I gave him a kiss and told him that his plan was perfectly reasonable. 'Not that I really want to be reasonable,' I added, 'but perhaps, under the circumstances, I have no real choice.'

'Precisely, my dear,' he answered, and that was the end of that.

So . . . we were at day two and counting. I read, I wrote, I ran, and I mustered the most extraordinary *mélange* of vegetables for dinner that mother nature has ever smiled upon. 'I've decided to do something different this evening,' I announced over cocktails. 'Enough fish, enough chicken!' I cried before we sat down to dinner. 'And certainly enough beef, veal, and lamb. It's time to pare down. It's time to face the organic facts of life. It's time to think about cholesterol and all of those other things that people our age don't have to think about yet.'

'Are you quite finished?' Desi asked.

'Yes, I think that I've got it all properly out of my system.'

'Murder, my sweet, is not quite the same thing as high cholesterol and high blood pressure and incipient diabetes. And, in all candor, it may not actually be murder. But my point is simply this: we need to tread lightly, and we need to trust each other along the way. Agreed?'

'Absolutely, Desi dearest. Please lead the way.'

And so he did. First to the living room, where we enjoyed a very private dinner dimly illuminated, and then upstairs where we — well, by now I trust that you have the general idea. I certainly did.

Wednesday, 3 October

I spent most of the following day — our chosen day of reckoning — back in my apartment: cleaning, paying bills, taking care of laundry and other mundane matters, trying to give the place a lived-in feeling once again. I couldn't stay in the carriage house forever, and I wanted to be able to feel at home back in my own little lair when the right moment arrived.

I also wanted to keep my mind off of Desi's dinner as much as possible. I left him to follow up on all of the details, as he had requested, and I happily agreed to be simply a special guest, appearing a little earlier than everyone else. I decided to dress down for the event — or at least somewhat soberly: a black blazer and skirt, black heels, and a deep red camisole under the short, tailored jacket. Whatever Dolores chose to wear for the evening, I was resolved to be appropriately demure for the occasion.

Six o'clock arrived almost before I was ready. I decided to brave the night air and walk up to Desi's house in my flats, changing into less sensible shoes once I was safely through the door.

And so I did. Not too many people were stirring, I soon realized: a waiter at the door, whom I did not recognize, and a number of other people in black tie — all male — ostensibly preparing the living room for a dinner for (almost) twelve.

I discovered Desi upstairs, in the bedroom, resplendent in a crisp navy suit, a white shirt with its customary cutaway collar, and a lovely tie whose various colors had been intricately intertwined. 'Just as martinis should be shaken,' he once explained to me, 'so ties should be woven. Not knit, mind you, but beautifully woven. Trust them to get it right in the Place Vendôme.'

'You look ready for battle,' I remarked.

'And so do you, my dear. I like the camisole: just the right touch.'

'Almost matronly, don't you think?'

'Nothing about you is ever matronly,' he replied, brushing a finger gently across my cheek. 'Least of all braless in a crimson camisole.

'Are you ready?' he added. 'You're going to need a seatbelt as well as a stiff drink.'

'Let's start with the drink,' I responded, 'and take it from there.'

We walked downstairs and took stock of the situation. Our guests would begin to arrive in a few minutes. The table was beautifully set. The waiters had glasses of wine and water on two trays, and a small bar had been set up in the kitchen. The *hors d'oeuvres* were simple but plentiful: shrimp, potstickers, chicken satay, and endive filled with a garlicky hummus. Dinner would be simple as well. Desi had decided to ask Jules to replicate our original meal on the island: lamb, carrots and rice, a tomato salad, ice cream to finish — if, in fact, we got that far.

I ordered a Cosmopolitan — and why not? Desi ordered a sparkling water with a slice of lime.

I instantly knew that it was going to be a long evening.

Renata was the first to arrive, God bless her, and she was noticeably warmer in demeanor when Desi gave her a kiss and asked what her pleasure would be. 'I'll have what the lady's having,' she quickly answered, and soon the two of us had our cranberry-tinged drinks in hand and the living room more or less to ourselves.

But not for long. Desi's guests had decided to be punctual, and within the next fifteen minutes we were joined by virtually everyone else: Jeremy (happy to see Renata once again), Richard (pleasant, I thought, but somewhat ill at ease), young Jack Springer (affectionate but polite), Andy Cameron (curious and quiet), and Madeleine and Dennis (pleased not to be the last to arrive). That honor belonged to John and Dolores, who entered the carriage house in high spirits, seemingly oblivious to the reason for this curious reunion. And I must admit that Dolores looked stunning — wrapped in a tightly fitting silk dress, her hair beautifully highlighted, her body nicely tanned from a recent trip somewhere south of Metuchen. And her shoes! Even I, official custodian of the Higginson Museum of Heels, felt more than a pang of covetousness. The combination of straps, studs, and loft would have been flattering to anyone, but even more so to the Voluptuous One. 'They're Italian, darling,' she whispered to me. 'They're called bondage shoes, but don't mention that to poor John; he already has enough ideas.'

Note to *moi-même*: find yourself your own consolation prize once this ordeal is over.

When everyone had a glass in hand, Desi quietly led those who had not visited the house before — Andy, Jack, Richard, and Jeremy (who had seen nothing but a sea of faces two weeks earlier) — back through the kitchen to the terrace, then up to the grand library on the second floor. Not to be outdone, John seized their departure as an opportunity to expound upon Desi's collection, assessing the particular strengths (and weaknesses) on display for the enlightenment of Madeleine, Dennis, Renata, Dolores, and myself, all of us bestowing smiles of gratitude upon our increasingly florid Englishman. When Desi and his small entourage returned, he and John engaged in an animated conversation about whether it would still be possible to purchase a first-rate Stubbs or Wright, something worthy of the Reynolds or Constable or Kauffman hanging on the walls. Desi remained skeptical. John, ever the self-promoting optimist, predicted that his friend would add one to his collection within three years — along with several other desiderata that he quickly ticked off without the least shred of compunction.

As usual, Desi took it all in stride and with good humor, taking advantage of John's effervescence and strong opinions in order to divert his guests' attention from the real issues at hand as long as he could. This strategy continued as we sat down to dinner. Instead of symbolically including a twelfth setting that would not be used, Desi simply arranged the left-hand side of the table with four chairs rather than five, placing everyone exactly where they were seated during our dinner in Sag Harbor. Was everyone aware of this? I couldn't imagine how they could *not* be, with the possible exception of John, of course, who was happily holding forth at my end of the table once again.

The first two courses were consumed as we talked one-on-one, Desi directing his attention to Renata and Dolores while I chatted with Andy and John. Our guests on each side of the table also held up their end of the bargain, largely due to the vigilance of Madeleine on my right and Jeremy and Dennis on my left. The atmosphere was convivial enough, if also somewhat subdued.

When it was time to turn to dessert, Desi gently tapped his spoon against his water glass and brought everyone to attention — including John. The waiters, led by a *maître d'* I had never seen before, quickly brought out coffee cups and someone else's homemade ice cream. As dessert and coffee were quietly served, our major domo removed the candlesticks, the flowers, and Desi's place setting from the table, installed a laptop and small projector in front of him, and then just as ably erected a white screen directly in back of where I was sitting. I was ready to move to the side, closer to Andy, but Desi flashed me a quick look that held me in place. We weren't quite ready for his slide show.

'I want to thank all of you for joining Abby and me this evening, and I especially want to thank those of you who rearranged your schedules so that this dinner could take place,' he began.

'When I invited you to join us, I did so in the spirit of trying to resolve the mystery surrounding our friend David Lundgren's untimely death. I can't say that I know with perfect certainty just how his death occurred. But I think that I know enough to share with you some observations and to ask some pertinent questions. To be clear, I haven't been deputized by the local police, although I've tried to work quite closely with them. My interests here are personal; I thought very highly of David and was very fond of him. But this is no vendetta. I have merely tried to help the police piece together what happened to David.'

Desi paused to take a sip of water.

'When the police began their investigation,' he continued, 'they naturally focused on the people David knew best: his colleagues at the museum, other friends and acquaintances in the art world, and then — most closely — the young men who had been his lovers during the past few years.'

Then, turning to Richard Yung halfway down the table, Desi added, 'and they naturally spent some time talking with Richard, who as you know had been David's lover and closest friend during the final two months or so of his life. The police have named him a "person of interest" in this case, as he obviously is. But they have not charged him with David's murder.

'Beyond Richard, however, they have not been able to identify anyone who might plausibly be linked by relationship, motive, or local circumstances to David's death. And so that's where I come in.'

Richard had been doing his best not to look incredibly uncomfortable. Now everyone else seemed to be imitating him.

'I began with a simple observation — and

then I let my intuition lead me where it would.

'When Abby and I retired to bed following our dinner together in Sag Harbor, I mentioned to her that I thought David had been uncharacteristically quiet that evening. Abby hadn't focused on this herself, but she didn't disagree with my remark. And so, when I began to think about whether our dinner party on the Island could have had anything to do with what happened just two or three days later, I naturally returned to my earlier sense that something had irritated or upset David. But I had no idea what could have provoked him — or who. At least not at that point.

'So I began by following the usual logical trails. Did he meet someone at Abby's party whom he found offensive? Did one of our guests do or say something directly to offend him? Or might it be more complicated than that?'

At this point Desi asked the head waiter to dim the lights a bit, and I moved my chair to the side so that I wouldn't be caught in the headlights of his projector.

'As a scholar, I told myself that I would be on much firmer ground with some corroborating evidence, but if I couldn't find that evidence among my fellow diners, where exactly was it likely to be discovered?

'Fortunately, as it turned out, technology — which has never been my closest ally — smiled upon me in the guise of Renata's new digital camera. I think that we were all aware that she had been trying out her new toy throughout the day, and by the time she was done, she had compiled a fairly large collection of images.'

'A hundred and sixty-three, to be precise,' Renata added, and a small tinkle of appreciative laughter spread around the table.

'And so Renata and I printed out all one hundred and sixty-three images, including the ones she would rather have erased from her camera's prodigious memory, and we carefully laid them out in chronological order. They offer, as you will see, remarkably full documentation of the long day we spent together.'

Desi clicked on the projector and hit the button on his laptop that began the slide show, which commenced with Renata's arrival on Saturday morning and concluded with her departure on Sunday.

In between was a parade of images making their way through the arrival of other guests, lunch by the pool, the visit to the beach, the discovery of Andy and Jack on my doorstep, drinks in the sitting rooms, drinks by the outdoor grill, Desi and me preparing dinner, and then the dinner itself, taken from various perspectives. Then two or three final photographs of the four young men as they took their late-night swim and a few shots of everyone at breakfast the next morning. All in all, I thought, a beautiful day nicely captured on film, as we used to say.

'Now,' Desi continued, 'I want to focus our attention on David alone.'

We didn't need Desi's commentary to interpret the twenty or so photographs we then saw as the projector — moving more slowly now — flashed its images of David over a period of roughly twenty-four hours.

Here was David somewhat anxiously introducing Richard to us, but obviously enjoying the moment nonetheless. Then a happy face at lunch, followed by the two young men in their skimpy swimsuits on the beach, followed in turn by a refreshed and nicely laundered David enjoying sauvignon blanc in the front rooms of Captain Logan's house.

Only during dinner did the storm clouds begin to emerge. The first sign was simply David's quiet, placid countenance between the smiling faces of Madeleine and John. Then David looking intently down the table in Desi's direction. Then a shot of him speaking, with animation returning to his face. Then the quiet and almost petulant look once again. A detail of David's face as the young men were about to take their swim revealed someone caught up in the fun of it, but the only photograph of him the following morning captured a quiet and contemplative countenance once again.

Desi allowed the final shot to linger for a number of seconds and then quietly said, 'This is roughly the last view I had of David — and for now, at least, this is how I shall remember him.'

Desi then turned the projector off but kept the lights slightly dimmed.

'So what was it that led to such a dramatic change within only an hour or two?' he asked.

Turning to Richard, who had barely raised his eyes from the table, Desi put a question to him as kindly as it was possible to do.

'Would you say, Richard, that the arrival of Andy had a complicated effect on how you and David were together that weekend?'

Richard and Andy looked warily at each other — and we, I suppose, looked just as warily at both of them. Seated between them, Jeremy diplomatically moved his chair a few inches backwards so they didn't have to lean forward to speak to each other — an unnecessary gesture, as it turned out, because Richard decided to address the entire table, and Desi in particular.

'I've told both Desmond and the police the same thing, which is that I very much enjoyed meeting Andy, that we exchanged phone numbers and email addresses with each other, and that we said we'd try to get together at some point. And I did give Andy a call on Monday, as I've now made clear.

'But I can honestly say that none of this,' he

continued, with more warmth in his voice, 'seemed to bother David. It was clear to me Sunday morning and then when we saw each other at the Met on Monday that he was upset about something, but he twice told me that I wasn't the cause. He might have been mildly irritated to start with, but then he saw Andy as someone both of us should get to know in due course. Whatever was bothering David, it wasn't Andy, and it wasn't me.'

'But,' Desi responded, 'isn't it true that we only have your word for it, Richard?'

'Yes.'

'And isn't it also true that you have lied both to the police and to me?'

This news quickly produced a rustle of excitement around the table.

'Yes, Desmond, I did. And I told both you and the police why I acted the way I did. I was scared. I was scared to death, and I didn't know what to do.'

'What, Richard,' Desi continued, 'was so frightening?'

Richard was trying hard to retain his composure, trying hard to concentrate on simple answers to simple questions.

'I realized, first of all, that, as David's lover, I would probably be viewed with suspicion by the police — and that I didn't have an alibi.'

'So you told us that you called David that

evening, and we've confirmed that.'

'Correct.'

'But you lied when you told us that you hadn't paid him a visit at or close to the time of his death on Tuesday evening.'

'That's true.'

'But the police eventually determined that you had in fact taken a taxi to his apartment building around eight o'clock?'

'Yes.'

'Were you able to enter his apartment?'

'Yes, I did.'

'How did you get in?'

'I had a key.'

'Did the police ask you if you had one?'

'Yes.'

'And did you tell them you did?'

'No.'

'Why not, Richard?' Desi asked, his voice suddenly softening in tenor.

'Because' – Richard's voice began to crack with emotion – 'because when I entered the apartment, I found David lying on the floor. And when I tried to pick him up, I realized that he was dead.'

Tears ran down his cheeks before he broke down and sobbed. I quietly moved over, put my hand on his shoulder, and handed him a napkin.

As I did so, John turned to Desi and, true to form, asked the logical, but brutal question.

215

'Forgive me for saying so, but having confessed to being at David's apartment and having already lied to the police, why have there been no charges? It seems a little irregular.'

Desi paused several seconds and then quietly said, 'They haven't charged Richard because they believe he is innocent. Not of lying, mind you — and not of panicking, of which he is clearly guilty. But not of killing David Lundgren.'

'Then who in the world,' John cried, 'do you think *did* kill him? Was it Andy here? Or Jack over there?'

'Neither Jack nor Andy killed David,' Desi calmly replied.

I could feel the tension at the table begin to relax slightly once everyone had taken this last statement in. I, for one, was certainly relieved. But then John continued again, his voice beginning to thunder: 'Now, now, Desmond, I'm no fool. Why are we gathered here if we don't know who is guilty of this terrible murder?'

'I need to ask you for your indulgence, John, as I lead you through this conversation in my own somewhat convoluted way. As it turned out, David didn't actually know the person who killed him.'

'And how,' John replied, but this time with at least some exertion of control, 'do you know that to be true?'

'Because,' Desi quietly responded, 'David told

216

me.'

These simple words sent another electric current around the table, silencing even John for several moments. And then he, in turn, responded to the softness in Desi's voice: 'And how, may I ask, did David tell you?'

'First, John, by betraying his emotions — and doing so in a consistent pattern that can be chronologically established and analyzed.'

Dead silence.

Addressing the entire table at this point, Desi returned to the subject of Renata's photographic gallery. 'The photographs that Renata took clearly tell us that David was happy when he arrived in Sag Harbor. That he was happy at lunch. That he was happy on the beach, and then happy later when we had our drinks. During dinner, however, the camera captured a smile on his face only once, as he was speaking, and the only time he spoke at any length was when he unraveled my little conundrum involving the collecting of sea glass. He was unusually introverted during the rest of the meal, both before he spoke and afterward.

'Therefore I draw the obvious conclusion that whatever attracted his attention and began to prey upon him did so during the dinner itself. Was this the point at which Richard and Andy had a chance to get to know each other?'

'No,' I quietly replied. 'Jack and Andy were attached to you directly before dinner, and David and Richard were with me in the front rooms.'

'And they didn't speak to each other at the table,' Jeremy remarked. 'I obviously sat between them, and I distinctly remember first talking to Andy and then to Richard. We never broke into a three-way conversation.'

'And so when did Andy and Richard finally have a chance to talk to each other?' Desi asked.

'After dinner,' Andy answered, 'before we went swimming and then over more wine afterwards.'

'And where were David and Jack?' Desi continued.

'They were with us part of the time,' Andy said, 'but they also spent some time apart, talking to each other.'

'Is that right, Jack?' Desi asked.

'Yes, Desmond. Mostly after our swim, before your supply of Bordeaux finally ran dry,' he answered.

There certainly were a lot of bottles in the recycling bin the next morning, I reminded myself.

'I have therefore concluded,' Desi went on, 'that whatever frisson may have been generated between Richard and Andy that Saturday night, it occurred after dinner rather than during it. Richard may still be lying to us about his conversations with David; he may still be lying to us about what happened when he reached David's apartment on Tuesday night . . .'

'I'm not, Desmond,' Richard quietly said.

'But it's clear to me,' Desi continued, 'that something else caught David's attention on Saturday evening. David was a good listener, and he heard something that seemed to disquiet him. Based on my study of the photographs, I first thought that he was focusing his attention on me. But the closer I looked at the images with Renata, especially those she took when she got up from the table and shot David, Madeleine, and Jack from the other side, the more I realized that David was staring intently not at me but at someone else. Wasn't he, Jack?'

'I'm not sure, Desmond,' Jack replied, slowly and carefully, as we all turned in his direction.

'I didn't notice it at the time.'

'Did you afterwards?' Desi asked.

'Not exactly. When we spoke after swimming, it was a fairly casual conversation. David wanted to know more about my dissertation, about my time at Oxford, and so forth.'

'Did he ask you about North Dakota?' Desi asked.

'He may have.'

'Did he tell you that he had relatives there?' Desi continued.

'No, he didn't.'

'What about later, when you spoke on the phone?'

Silence.

'And what about Tuesday evening, when you visited him at his apartment?'

'What makes you think I went to see him?' Jack replied.

'David told me so.'

'What do you mean he told you so?'

Taking a folded sheet of paper from the inside pocket of his suit jacket, Desi looked again at Jack before addressing all of us around the table. 'Earlier that evening, David decided to send himself an email. He did so not on his museum account, but on a personal email service to which he subscribed. When the message arrived a few seconds later, he deleted it. But it was safely banked somewhere in the ether, as he well knew. All he (or we) needed to do was to look under "sent" messages.'

Desi paused for a few seconds before continuing. 'This was his subject line: "Unmasking Jack Springer."'

Once again there was palpable movement around the table. Jack's face remained rigid as he continued to stare at Desi.

'And here is David's message to himself,' Desi continued: 'On Saturday I met someone called Jack Springer when I stayed with friends in Sag Harbor.

'Although I'm related to Springers on my mother's side, I didn't pay any attention to his name until, at dinner, he said something about coming from North Dakota. I then remembered that he had also attended Oxford. This seemed like a strange coincidence, for I had a second cousin in North Dakota named Bill Springer who had won a fellowship to Oxford about seven years ago.

'Bill was killed in a car crash a few weeks before he was to leave. I had met him only once or twice, I think, when we were younger, but my mother had stayed in touch and drove out to the funeral from Minneapolis. When Jack and I talked later in the evening, I discovered that he grew up in the same town as my cousin, although I didn't say anything about Bill.

'On Sunday, when I returned to New York, I talked with my mother on the phone. I didn't want to upset her in any way, but I did ask her for some genealogical information, and I learned that my cousin's full name was William Jackson Springer. Mine, of course, is David Jackson Lundgren.

'This looked odd, to say the least, so on Monday I checked the website for Columbia's art history department, but I couldn't find Jack's name anywhere. I then remembered that he was teaching at the Fashion Institute, and there it was: "Introduction to European Portraiture. Instructor: W. Jackson Springer."

'I had Jack and Andy's phone numbers and finally decided to call Jack last night. He was happy to hear from me until I told him why I was calling. At first he refused even to talk about it, but eventually he agreed to get together with me later tonight. He insisted on coming here. Not a good idea, I think, but I couldn't get him to agree to an alternative and I'm not sure that I should involve anybody else. In any case, I'm sending this note to myself. More later.'

Desi stopped, looked up at Jack, and waited for a response. He got none, but I could see the veins and muscles flexing in Jack's neck.

Finally Jack angrily asked, 'How do I know that this email is for real?'

Desi turned the projector back on and hit a key. There, on the screen, was David's entire message, sent to himself at seven in the evening.

Desi then turned to the *maître d'* once more and asked him to approach the table.

'Our head waiter this evening is named Alphonse Lafargue. Mr. Lafargue is also a private detective. He has verified the fact that William Jackson Springer was killed in an automobile accident in North Dakota a little more than seven years ago. He has also verified the fact that, immediately after that accident, W. Jackson Springer matriculated at one of Oxford's colleges, with a scholarship for two years of tuition.'

I was suddenly aware that the rest of the waiters had quietly made their way from the kitchen and were discreetly lined up near the entrance to the living room.

Desi looked once again at Jack and asked him, 'Who was responsible for the death of David Lundgren?'

Jack looked around the table at us, dropped his head, and said, 'Douglas Parker.'

'And who is Douglas Parker?'

'*I* am Doug Parker,' he softly murmured, sounding defeated. 'But I never meant to hurt David. He pressed me again and again about Bill, never letting me explain. And when I tried to leave, he blocked the door. And so I shoved him aside — and he fell. And that, that was it. So fast, so simple, so stupid.'

Desi rose and walked over to him. 'There are no policemen here, Doug,' he said. 'But Sergeant Mullins is waiting for you outside.'

Desi slowly led him across the living room, past the waiters, but before they left through the door to the street beyond, Doug swung around and cried, 'It was an accident! All of it. None of this would have happened . . .'

I slowly looked around and saw the look of shock on everyone's face. But no one was more shocked than I was.

Wednesday – Friday, 3-5 October

Desi returned about twenty minutes later. During his absence the waiters had cleared the table, taken away the laptop and projector, and reappeared with a selection of port and single-malt Scotches. Our guests took a quick drink and then made their *adieux* slowly and graciously, each giving me a hug, each saying how relieved they were that this unfortunate affair was over. Especially Richard, who looked not only relieved but downright dazed as Andy took him by the arm and led him out the door. Monsieur Lafargue had left earlier, quickly following Desi and Jack — yes, I'll simply call him Jack, I think — and once the waiters took their leave, that left only me, Dennis, and Madeleine, whom (I learned) Desi had asked to stay behind until he returned.

Once he was safely in the door and our friends had departed, he took me in his arms, kissed my cheek, and suggested that all verbal explanations be put on hold until both of us had fully recovered. 'I need a drink,' he quietly announced, 'and you need one of Dr. Fairbrother's famous sleeping pills.' I readily agreed to both propositions.

And although tomorrow was, of course, another day, we decided the following morning to continue our verbal armistice. I returned to my apartment, took a long run and a hot shower, did some shopping in the neighborhood, and made discreet inquiries about a certain pair of studded black heels that would find a very welcome home in one of my tiny closets. Desi stopped by at seven, admired what he saw – including the small Homer that now graced one of the walls — and took me out for an old-fashioned peasant dinner at our little bistro. Roast chicken and potatoes, haricots verts, a luscious Grand Marnier soufflé to follow; crisp Alsatian wine as an aperitif, an expensive bottle of Crozes Hermitage for the main course, and a glass of old Armagnac to round everything off. There's nothing like comfort food from the *campagne* when one is really in need of comfort. And both of us certainly were.

I spent the night *chez moi* for the first time in a week, sleeping like a baby and ready to chase those shoes the minute the stores opened Friday morning. Our plan was for me to join Desi for a postmortem at the carriage house that evening. He promised to give me a full wrap-up and an exotic dinner as well. On the second floor, no less. Only Desi would think of that as exotic — but then only Desi has a library that would seat twenty in a pinch.

I suppose that I'm as wedded to retail therapy as anyone I know. But I'm also a New Englander, and New Englanders — as the old adage goes — don't buy their hats, they *have* their hats. And their houses, and their cars, and their boats, and even their shoes! I suppose that I still grudgingly admire the way in which my mother and father (and even more so their own parents before them) proudly announced just how old their things were, how beautifully they had weathered, how often they had been mended. It's Yankee chic, along with drafty houses and cold-roast Boston and a climate that is just as unforgiving.

I suppose it took those wonderful years in Paris to wean me from my crusty heritage. And yet my version of retail therapy is not quite that of most New Yorkers. I'm not always underfoot at the sales or darkening the doors of those interesting little shops in mid-town that will sell you remnants of the latest fabrics from Paris or Milan. My brand of retail therapy is very simple: I only buy the best that I can afford (and sometimes just a little beyond what I can afford). And I've never looked back with buyer's regret — only with non-buyer's remorse. Sometimes the very best comes in small and affordable portions, such as the chocolates produced by my favorite *chocolatier* on Madison. But today I had my sights on something rather more substantial, and if I were successful in my hunt, then I had other purchases to make as well.

By the time I had lugged my person and my packages back to the cocoon, it was rather late in the afternoon and I had two messages on my machine. The first was from Desi, suggesting that I come half an hour later than planned; the second was from Renata, who was ready for a girls' lunch out. I acknowledged both calls, listened to some of my favorite Haydn piano sonatas while I unpacked and tidied up, and then reconsidered my attire for the evening. It was just the two of us and I wanted to get it right.

When, an hour later, Desi took my coat and gave me his usual once-over, I immediately knew that I had gotten it right. No cat calls or whistles in Desmond Fairbrother's world, mind you, but he does have a tendency to produce a rather sweet 'hmmm' when he likes what he sees. I got a very long 'hmmm' and a very appreciative kiss.

'You've outdone yourself, Abby.'

'So you remember,' I said, 'that the Voluptuous One sported these shoes just two nights ago?'

'Hard to forget, my dear, even considering the circumstances.'

'They have the cutest name, Desi: they're

called "bondage shoes," although Dolores doesn't want her poor John in on the secret.'

'I promise to keep your indiscretions to myself. You must have visited every S&M shop in the Village to find just the right accessories.'

'Not *every* shop, darling, just a few. Once I produced the shoes, the salesmen were only too happy to ply me with their various wares. There's nothing so basic, one of them told me, as black leather with chrome studs: "it's a real classic."'

'I'm almost speechless, my dear,' Desi replied. 'Just let me take another good look at you.'

And so he did as we walked to the kitchen, admiring the studded leather bracelets, the matching belt, and the black leather choker with its rows of sharp pyramids — with a black miniskirt and skintight halter-top serving as the perfect foils.

'You're only missing a dog leash,' he said at last.

'How do you know that I don't have one in my handbag?' I countered. 'And how does a girl get a drink around here, anyway?'

'What are you into, as my Australian friends like to say?'

'I'm into vintage champagne, the good stuff.'

'I only serve the good stuff.'

'Then I want the *really* good stuff. And the nice old flutes. *Pronto*!'

Desi kissed me once again and quickly went

to work, picking out the best Edwardian flutes (rather rare, I think) and a bottle of champers from the wine cooler that had just the right label on it — and just the right year.

We drank, we jousted, and we drank again. What next, I thought? 'More, please — *pronto*!'

What followed was a genuine surprise, however. Desi quietly led me upstairs and over to the double doors that open onto the library at the front of the house. Both doors were completely closed. Something was clearly afoot.

I've probably spent as much time working in Desi's library as he has; it's simply one of the world's most pleasant places to read, to write, to talk, or to daydream. And we've used it for a few other purposes as well.

The library's footprint is almost as large as that of the living room below it, but whereas every other space in the carriage house is serene and fastidiously edited, this wonderful room is a veritable riot of color and material culture. Three tall windows look out onto the street below, with small comfortable chairs taking advantage of the natural light. On each side of the central window is an antique writing table, one devoted to Desi's research, the other to more practical affairs. Large, formal bookcases have been placed against the walls to the left and right as you enter, with slightly smaller versions of the same bookcases framing the double doors behind you.

The bookcases have been painted a rich cream color, with natural mahogany shelving and gold leaf picking out the intricate details. They are all completely filled — the shelves above, the cabinets below — with Desi's working collection of catalogues and monographs, and with handsome French boxes containing the records of his various ventures.

The walls of this large rectangular room have been lined with a dark green moiré silk, against which Desi has hung his collection of eighteenth- and early nineteenth-century French portraits, all executed in pastel and mounted in hand-rubbed gold-leaf frames. Combinations of small tables and chairs have been arranged in front of the various bookcases, but the room itself is anchored by an oversized Heriz rug, two large Chesterfield sofas filled with colorful pillows, a Venetian chandelier hanging from the ceiling, and an oversized glass coffee table in the very center of the library, groaning (if plate glass can be said to groan) under its burden of books, dealers' catalogues, magazines, and manuscripts in various stages of draft or proof.

This was the warm and welcoming environment in which I imagined we were about to enjoy dinner. But not exactly so, as it turned out, for Desi had literally turned the tables on me once again.

He began by knocking on one of the two

mahogany doors. Both were soon pulled open by young male waiters dressed in dinner jackets and black tie.

'Oh my God,' I murmured. 'I think I received the wrong dress code for this evening.' And then, as I looked rather more carefully into the room: 'At least you don't have Patricia Simmons ensconced in one of the sofas.'

'All in good time, my dear. As for your attire, you may be right: it may not be entirely appropriate for the rest of the evening. I have a change of clothing ready for you as well as for me. It's time, I think, to take that weapon of mass destruction off your beautiful neck. Jules has arrived, by the way, and has started making final preparations for our dinner.'

'All of this fuss just for the two of us? Why not invite several of our friends as well?'

'Soon enough, old girl. But we need to have some time together first. You have questions to ask, and I have answers to give.'

'Fair enough,' I agreed as I began to take in the major change in the room, which entailed removing the central glass table and placing a lovely round antique table in its place — just large enough for the two of us and a panoply of bottles, china, silverware, and glasses, with a beautiful bouquet of deeply tinted salmon roses on the side. And next to the flowers, I wasn't too surprised to discover, was the beautiful little painting by Thomas Jones, sitting happily on a small bronze easel.

One of the waiters dimmed the lights, lit the candles, and poured us two glasses of what looked unmistakably like Puligny-Montrachet. It tasted like it, too.

'If we take a moment to walk back to the bedroom,' Desi said, 'there are a few items waiting for you in the closet.'

'Interesting, Desi,' I replied. 'I'm not sure whether I'm suddenly on a magical mystery tour or trapped within one of those vintage *Avengers* shows: you know, "House of Cards" or something like that.'

'If you say so,' he responded, as if he couldn't firmly place Steed and Mrs. Peel on his private cultural map.

He had, however, chosen with care: silver silk trousers (which would work perfectly with my new shoes), one of those white cotton blouses his shirtmaker had made for me, and a small black box that he placed in my hands.

'I'll put on my dinner jacket,' Desi said, 'and then you can open the box before we return to the library.'

'It's a deal,' I said, exchanging my tight-fitting top and skirt for the casual, tailored black-tie look. When I was done, I sat on the bed holding the beautiful little jewelry box in both hands.

'A little gift, Abby. Wear them with

happiness.'

I opened the box and discovered two beautiful enamel-and-gold cufflinks in the shape of elegant ladybugs. The combination of the rich gold with the red and black enamel was dazzling, and even I could deftly maneuver each link into its proper place at the center of a perfectly starched cuff.

'You are very, very bad, Desi,' I told him. 'Please continue to be this bad for a very long time.'

'That's an easy promise to keep,' he said as he received my extended kiss. 'It's not every girl, after all, who would swoon over a pair of cufflinks that match her economy convertible.'

'It's not an economy car,' I replied. 'It's a sophisticated sports car disguised as a golf cart.'

We sat down on one of the beautifully tufted Chesterfields and admired the warm *hors d'oeuvres* that suddenly appeared on small silver salvers. Music had been turned on in the background and the entire room glowed in the candlelight. Our putative European ancestors looked down, rather intelligently I thought, from their perches on those handsomely decorated walls, and the spines of several thousand books conspired to lend the space a sense of warmth as well as order.

Desi smiled, almost as if he could read my thoughts.

'Yes,' he said, 'it's a pretty nice room — a

very comforting room, I think. And Jules has some interesting surprises for us this evening.'

'For us?' I asked. 'Don't you know what he's serving?'

'No; it's entirely up to him. I simply said that we had had enough lamb and carrots — and ice cream! — and that whatever he wanted to prepare would certainly be more than acceptable.'

More than acceptable, indeed. But as one lovely morsel succeeded another — and even more so as we sat down to dinner with a bottle of Burgundy whose name I'm afraid I can't remember, although I certainly should — our conversation inevitably focused on the ordeal we had recently been through. Desi was ready to deliver, and I was more than ready to inquire, cajole, and punctuate.

'Can we still call him Jack?' I began.

'If you wish.'

'And do you think he told us the truth two nights ago?'

'I have no reason to doubt it, but it will be up to the authorities — and eventually to a jury — to decide how to charge him and then how to judge him. We don't know of any previous episode of violence. He seems, if anything, to be a young man with a remarkable amount of self-control.'

'Do you think he would have harmed me if I had opened the door to my apartment and stepped inside?'

'But that's just the point, Abby: he left as soon as he heard you put your keys in the lock. If he had intended any violence, he would have stayed.'

I thought about that for a moment.

'Why do you think he broke into the apartment in the first place?'

'That question has puzzled me a good deal, and I'm still not entirely sure. My first response was that someone was trying to send us a signal, a threat: leave well enough alone. Or, alternatively, I later wondered whether Jack was checking to see whether David had shared his thoughts with you, which might be found either in your laptop or in your notebook. You might even have written something there yourself. You *are* the designated writer, my dear.'

'Thanks a lot!'

'Either that, or because he's infatuated with you. Don't forget that you turned him down that evening. He might have acted on instinct. Whatever it was, he made a big mistake.'

I wasn't much comforted by the idea.

'In any case, it didn't make any difference because the break-in convinced me that only someone close to us would have done it and, convinced that it was someone we knew, I decided to press Lafargue even harder to see if he could find a link between David and someone at our party — someone other than Richard, of course.'

'And he did.'

'Yes, he did, but it took him a long time to do so. The trail was very thin, and over seven years had passed since Doug Parker had taken on Bill Springer's identity. I, in fact, was the one who began the legwork by asking David's father whether he had heard of any of our guests that weekend, and he hadn't, of course. Had I talked with David's mother — and had I mentioned the small town in North Dakota — I might have gotten somewhere, but it's clear that even David's mother didn't tumble to things as quickly as David himself did. But then he always had an eye for detail.'

'So how did you find the trail?'

'I asked Lafargue to talk with both of David's parents. Once we knew that there was a Springer connection of some kind in North Dakota, he then tried to track down the Springers, but that, too, was difficult. Bill was virtually an only child of older parents; he had one older sister, but she had married and moved away years and years ago. The Springers decided to move to Arizona after Bill's accident, and only Mrs. Springer is still living; she's in her early nineties, and it took a lot of work to find her.'

'Still *compos mentis*?'

'Pretty much so. It's clear that she and her husband were devastated by their son's sudden death. They couldn't face handling all of the details themselves, so they naturally asked Bill's friend from high school, Doug Parker, if he would help them. They asked him to be in touch with Bill's college at Oxford to explain what had happened; he also said that he would contact the foundation in New York that had awarded Bill the scholarship.'

'Had Bill and Doug stayed in touch?'

'Very much so. Doug was orphaned very early on and lived with his maternal grandmother. He attended the state university, majoring in history, just as Bill did at a private college in Ohio. Bill had the entire world before him; Doug had a teaching job lined up at a high school in South Dakota. And so . . .'

'Yes, Desi, and so . . . All Doug needed to do was step into his friend's shoes and escape.'

'Those dear, all-trusting Midwesterners,' Desi cried, with a smile. 'They gave Doug the entire file labeled "Oxford," which contained Bill's passport, his letter of introduction from the foundation to the college, his college transcript, and a one-way plane ticket from Minneapolis to London. All Doug needed to do was alter Bill's name slightly, change the passport photo, make a lateral move into art history, write a letter each year to the foundation, and earn enough money doing odd jobs to keep himself afloat. And then when he began to excel at rowing as well as art history, he found himself an undergraduate celebrity within his college.'

'No one else there from Bill's undergraduate college?'

'Apparently not, and that was a stroke of luck for Jack, if we're now going to call him that.'

'And his grandmother?'

'She died during his first year in England.'

'And the Springers?'

'They may not have expected to hear from him once he moved away to take up his teaching job somewhere in South Dakota.'

'And after Oxford, Columbia was a large university in one of the largest cities in the world.'

'Yes, New York probably provided him with more camouflage than any other place he could have chosen. But,' Desi added, 'time finally caught up with him in Sag Harbor.'

'And that's why he's called the subtle thief.'

'Who?'

'Back to our regicide poet, Desi. Time, Milton told us, is the subtle thief of youth.'

'Ah yes,' Desi replied. 'And time ran out for Jack Springer over dinner in Captain Logan's house on a Saturday evening in mid-September of this year.'

I paused for half a minute or so.

'How, Desi, did you ever find the email that David wrote to himself?'

'Ah, that was the most difficult part of the entire puzzle — and that's why I kept asking questions about laptops and on-line auctions.'

'I don't follow you,' I said.

'In the good old days, when the Sam Spades of this world wanted to place incriminating evidence in a safe place, they sealed the information in an envelope and mailed it to themselves. Do you remember?'

'I do.'

'So I asked myself whether David, who was a very methodical young man, might have done so as well. If he had, it was likely that he emailed it to himself, but there was no trace of such a message on his computer at work. So knowing that he almost certainly followed the on-line auctions, I suspected that he did so at home by using an email service that he personally subscribed to. Lafargue and I persuaded the police that it was worth checking David's credit-card statements to see if there was a monthly charge, and we found it. All that needed to happen after that was for the police to gain access to his account via the provider. Once we had that, it didn't take long to find the email.'

'But that email alone didn't prove that Jack actually visited David that evening, did it?' I asked.

'No, you're absolutely right, and that's why Mullins allowed me to use the email as a way of seeing whether Jack would confess to visiting David, which could otherwise be difficult to prove.'

'But why did David pursue him so relentlessly that evening, if we can believe what Jack has told us?'

'Because David was still in many ways a very conservative person — a real straight-arrow, as we used to say. He probably felt that Jack had acted both illegally and immorally.'

'What will happen to Jack now, do you think?' I asked.

'Where do I start? With your apartment? The window has been fixed, you won't press any charges, and your notebook and computer are sitting over there on my table.'

'Oh my God, Desi. You *have* been busy.'

'Yes, it's been a productive two days.'

'What about identity theft?'

'The old-fashioned kind? That's up to the authorities, whoever they may turn out to be. But I spoke with the elderly Mrs. Springer, and she says that she's actually pleased that Bill's opportunity to study at Oxford didn't go to waste.'

'Don't you just love those Midwesterners?' I cooed.

'As for the foundation here in town, I know one of the trustees and I don't think that they will pursue it. I doubt whether Jack's college at

Oxford will either. They've countenanced much worse in the past thousand years — and he did row in their first boat, remember.'

'But Columbia?' I asked.

'Yes, Jack faces a problem up at Morningside Heights, but right now he faces a much larger problem downtown, where our friends must decide whether to charge him with manslaughter or some lesser felony. He does, however, have a very good attorney.'

'And who's paying for this very good attorney, anyway?'

'Let's just say that sympathetic lawyers like a good *pro bono* case when they see one.'

'My goodness, you *have* been busy. No wonder Jules has been cooking this evening rather than you.'

'And I must rise early in the morning as well. I have a full day tomorrow, too.'

'Doing what, exactly?'

'Preparing for class next week.'

'Which class?'

'Introduction to European portraiture, of course. Someone has to finish the semester, and it's the least I could do, under the circumstances.' I looked at him through the candlelight across the table and then rose from my chair and stood behind him, slowly running my hands through his wavy blond hair.

'Do you remember,' I asked, 'what Nick

Charles says to Nora at the end of *The Thin Man*?'

'The film or the novel?'

'The novel, of course!'

'No, Abby, I don't. In fact I've never read it, I'm ashamed to say.'

'So you should be. In any case, Nick says something like "Murder doesn't round out anybody's life except the person who's been murdered — and sometimes the murderer's."'

'That's nicely put,' he said. 'And of course it leaves the rest of us with the messy emotional aftermath, even if it wasn't murder.'

Desi moved his chair away from the table and I seated myself in his lap, facing him and continuing to play with his hair.

'Precisely,' I replied. 'That was Nora's response: "it's all pretty unsatisfactory." End of story.'

'And so it is — very unsatisfactory. Unless, of course, with time, we attempt to inscribe some kind of order upon it.'

'Ah, Desi, that's what the novelist does.'

'Or the historian.'

'No, my dear. This complicated tale belongs to the novelist.'

'You wouldn't dare!'

'And why not? You solved the mystery, you brought the culprit to justice, and I'm sure that you've provided some sense of solace to David's family. At least they know how much you admired and cared for him.'

'Can't we just leave it at that?'

'Perhaps, Dr. Fairbrother. Perhaps. But I reserve my rights. They may just come in handy some day.'

Author profile

Richard Wendorf is a literary and art historian who has served as Director of the American Museum & Gardens in Bath, Harvard's Houghton Library, and the Boston Athenaeum. He began his career as Professor of English and of Art History at Northwestern University. Educated at Williams College, Oxford, and Princeton, he is active in the cultural life of Bath and London.

Wendorf received the Annibel Jenkins Biography Prize for *Sir Joshua Reynolds: The Painter in Society* (Harvard and the NPG). He is also the author of *The Elements of Life* (Oxford), *After Sir Joshua* (Yale), *Printing History and Cultural Change* (Oxford), and *Growing Up Bookish: An Anglo-American Memoir* (Oak Knoll). This is his first novel.